CHERI-BIBI

CHERI-BIBI

A drama in 9 scenes by
Alevy and Marcel Nadaud
from the novel by
Gaston Leroux

translated and adapted by
Frank J. Morlock

A Black Coat Press Book

Gaston Leroux the Magician

In March of 1921, Alexandre Millerand, President of the French Republic, went to Marseilles for a state dinner. On leaving the train, Millerand and each of his companions, as well as the Mayor of Marseilles and other city officials, inexplicably found in their pockets a playing card: the seven of clubs.

Despite questioning and a thorough police investigation, the mystery remained unsolved until the following week. At that time, a Parisian newspaper announced the publication of the latest adventure novel of Gaston Leroux: *The Seven of Clubs*! It had all been a clever publicity ploy. This utilization of reality to enhance fantasy was an artifice typical of Leroux, a former journalist.

The author of *The Phantom of the Opera*, his best known book, was born in Paris in 1868, in a bourgeois family. Leroux was an excellent student, collecting all class honors, including swimming. One of his teachers is reputed to have told him that he would become either a writer or an attorney. He chose both. In 1890, he joined the Paris Bar as an *Avocat-Stagiaire* (attorney-in-training) while, at the same time, publishing poetry and short stories in various magazines.

Three years later, Leroux left the legal profession to work for the newspaper *Le Matin*. Because of his background, he was assigned to cover criminal matters. In the course of his work, he attended five state executions. The sight of the guillotine in action was one that was not easily forgotten. This experience was later useful in his fiction writing, which often featured passionate crime, courtroom drama and their sometimes frightful conclusions.

In 1896, Leroux was among the six reporters who accompanied President Felix Faure to Russia. Over the next few years, Leroux began to expand his field of coverage. He wrote about the Dreyfus Affair, French politics and his travels. In 1901, he published a first collection of his articles, *Sur Mon Chemin* (*On My Path*).

His first novel, *La Double Vie de Theophraste Longuet* (*The Double Life of Theophraste Longuet*), appeared in *Le Matin* in 1903. In it, Theophraste Longuet, a meek, mild-mannered bourgeois literally relives the life of Cartouche, the famous 18th century French bandit, and dies his horrible death–Cartouche was quartered.

La Double Vie reflected Leroux's fascination for the occult, and his knowledge of the criminal mind. It also exhibited his penchant for a certain *grand-guignol*. In it, a butcher's head is served in the same manner as a lamb's. Fantasy is also very much present since Theophraste encounters in the catacombs a civilization of twenty-fingered men speaking a 14th century French dialect.

In a stunt that has been imitated since, Leroux involved his readers in a treasure hunt. Clues had been planted in the novel, that would eventually enable someone to collect 25,000 francs.

For the next two years, Leroux became *Le Matin*'s correspondent in Russia. Aware of the cruelty and incompetence of the Tsarist regime, he was among the first to forecast the Russian Revolution. Throughout 1905, he covered tragic happenings, including such famous events as the Potemkin Revolt and the "Red Week" in Moscow.

In 1906, he returned to France where he wrote *Le ystère de la Chambre Jaune* (*The Mystery of the Yellow Room*). This launched his career as a writer. The book introduced the character of Joseph Rouletabille, a young enterprising journalist, whose powers of deduction rivaled those of Sherlock Holmes.

Rouletabille is, in France, one of the most famous detectives in popular fiction. In fact, his name has become a synonym for a spirit of cleverness and deduction. Rouletabille, along with two other French pulp heroes, Arsène Lupin and Fantômas, has inspired many film-makers. There were at least five movie adaptations of *The Mystery of the Yellow Room* between 1913 and 1965.

The Mystery of the Yellow Room is full of gothic atmosphere and, despite the rational explanation provided at the end, leaves many questions unanswered. Because of this, and of the book's success, Leroux wrote a sequel the following year, *Le Parfum de la Dame en Noir* (*The Scent of the Lady in Black*).[1]

The *Rouletabille* series continued until Leroux's death in 1927. Afterwards, two more Rouletabille novels were written by Noré Brunel. The *Rouletabille* novels contain a good share of fantasy elements, even though they are usually explained away by the hero in the end. Their supernatural apparitions, ghosts and magic are only the trappings of premeditated murder. However, it was in his other works that Leroux's talent for the macabre truly blossomed.

Because he was a journalist, Gaston Leroux wrote his novels as if they were fact. He often gave the exact dates of the events that he was narrating, and sometimes drew maps of the places involved (as in *The Mystery of the Yellow Room*). Several items reported by Leroux in his Russian articles found their way, almost word for word, in *Rouletabille and the Tsar*. Ballmeyer, Rouletabille's father, and the villain in *The Scent of the Lady in Black*, was based on the real-life international criminal Allmeyer, whose exploits were reported in *Le Figaro* the same year.

A characteristic of journalistic style is to place an emphasis on the sensational. That trait was particularly apparent in Leroux's fiction. Both his subjects and his techniques of narration were larger-than-life. One of Leroux's trademarks, for example, was the use of small, italicized phrases, such as:

---

[1] More information about *Rouletabille* can be found in our book *Shadowmen* (ISBN 0-9740711-3-7) also available from Black Coat Press.

"The dwarf saluted Mr. Baptiste *with one of his left hands*."

"Did the Gypsies steal you from your parents?" "No. *It was my parents who stole me from the Gypsies!*"

"That which he did not understand was that *they replaced the brain of a madman with that of a murderer!*"

"*It is not because you cut a woman in pieces and put her in our stove that you have killed her!*"

"Why is it that an honest clock *strikes midnight at a quarter past two?*"

With these italicized poems in prose, Leroux transformed reality into something truly bizarre. Their frequent usage added a poetic atmosphere to his work. They also were a perfect instrument to bring out the fantasy and horror of his themes.

Leroux wrote thirty-three novels during his career. Most of them today are considered classics in the genre. *The Phantom of the Opera* (1910) [2] presents the truly unforgettable character of Erik. Artist and Magician, Erik lives in the fantastic world that exists beneath the Paris Opera, which he built in part. Because of its larger-than-life characters and its completely surrealistic decor, the book has made a profound impression on all who have read it. *The Phantom of the Opera* has had

---

[2] Available in a Black Coat Press edition (ISBN 978-1-932983-13-5).

many film incarnations. The first, and perhaps the best, was in 1925, with Lon Chaney, Sr. in the role of Erik.

Leroux's style carries such conviction that it is hard to believe that he is not reporting real events. As late as 1972, an English woman wrote to the heirs of Leroux to let them know that she intended to discover the secret hiding place where Erik had left his final opera, *Don Juan Triumphant*.

In *La Poupée Sanglante* (*The Bleeding Puppet*) and *La Machine à Assassiner* (*The Killing Machine*) (both 1923), Leroux introduced the character of Gabriel, a humanoid robot. When the protagonist, Benedict Masson, wrongly accused of the murders of several young girls, is guillotined, Gabriel's inventor arranges to have Benedict's brain transplanted into Gabriel's body. Thus, Benedict can return to unmask and destroy the true killer, a vampire nobleman.

Le Fauteuil Hanté (*The Haunted Chair*) (1910) features a mad scientist who uses ultrasound and ultraviolet light to kill three academicians who discovered his secret. It is his demented son that he has imprisoned, and not himself, who is the real genius and inventor.

The mysteries of Mayerling and the secrets of the Gypsies are the subjects of two novels, *La Reine du Sabbat* (*The Queen of the Sabbath*) (1910) and *Rouletabille and the Gypsies* (1922). In both, Gaston Leroux showed that World War I was caused in part by feuding clans of Gypsies. The strange cultural traditions of the Romani are explored in such detail by Leroux that it is almost possible to believe that he was one of them.

Among the other themes explored by Leroux are undersea battles in *La Bataille Invisible* (*The Invisible Battle*) (1917), an underground king of the Parisian Underworld in *Le Roi Mystère* (*King Mystery*) (1908), dedicated to his "master," Alexandre Dumas, and an intelligent primate who is the missing link between ape and man in *Balaoo* (1911).

To impress his readers, Leroux often used elements of horror, such as dismemberment and graphic depictions of various tortures. In *Les Mohicans de Babel* (1926), he describes the *Torture of the 10,000 Pieces*:

"In clipped phrases, he announced what he was about to do. I heard him say: 'I first remove the muscles from the anterior face of the left arm.' Ah! It was well done! The flesh came off with the scalpel, just like a ribbon! 'Second, *ditto* with the right arm!' This *ditto* seemed more horrible to me than the most horrible of screams..."

The sight of the torture is followed by an even more terrifying spectacle. The hero beholds the corpses of the victims, "their mouths open, huge, like in theatrical masks," in a secret graveyard underneath the Seine.

Leroux's journalistic talents did not stop at these visual horrors. He knew, as perhaps no one else in his day, how to draw on reality to enhance his fiction. Through the clever inclusion of footnotes, or verifiable facts (i.e. events reported in the papers), he created the illusion of reality.

The Phantom of the Opera, *The Queen of the Sabbath* and several *Rouletabille* stories, contained names or occurrences that truly existed. The Opera's chandelier really did crash. The Queen of the Sabbath really did exist. With Leroux, you are never sure where reality stops and fantasy begins.

Jean-Marc & Randy Lofficier

GASTON LEROUX

CHÉRI-BIBI

Characters

Jean Mascart a.k.a. Chéri-Bibi
Cécile Bourrelier a.k.a. Cécily

in order of appearance:
La Ficelle (*Stringer*)
Marquis du Touchais
Marquise du Touchais
Maxime du Touchais, their son
Monsieur Bourrelier, Cécily's father
Reine
George de Pont-Marie, Maxime's friend
Jacqueline Mascart, Chéri-Bibi's sister, later Sister Mary of the Angels
Sergeant, later Inspector, Costaud (*Slugger*) of the Dieppe police force
Captain Barrachon of the *Bayard*
Lieutenant de Vilène of the *Bayard*
Chief Guard Pascaud of the *Bayard*
Gueule-de-Bois (*Woodface*), a convict
Petit-Bon-Dieu (*Baby Jesus*), a convict
Le Rouquin (*Red Hair*), a convict
Le Kanak, a convict, indigenous of New Caledonia, and a former surgeon
The Countess, le Kanak's girl-friend
Baron Proskoff
Nadja de Valrieu
Carmen de Fontainebleau
Petit Bernard
Sonia, Baroness Proskoff
Toinette, a dancing girl

and a variety of:
Servants
Police Officers
Peasants
Convicts
Guards
Sailors
Waiters, Maître D's
Dancers of both sexes

The action takes place in 1913.

The authors recommend that the actor playing Maxime du Touchais should have approximately the same weight and build as Chéri-Bibi.

SCENE I
THE MAN WITH THE GREY HAT

This is a prologue that takes place eight years prior to the rest of the play.

We are at the Chateau du Touchais, at Puys, near Dieppe, on a nice summer evening. On one side, we see the facade of the Chateau with a park at the rear; a stairway connects a terrace with some garden furniture to the park, and two French doors give access from the terrace to the interior of the Chateau. A window located just above ground on the terrace belongs to the kitchen, which is in the basement.

AT RISE, a servant comes down the stairway from the terrace. He goes to the kitchen window and calls:

SERVANT: La Ficelle! [3]

LA FICELLE: (*inside*) Here!

SERVANT: Pass me some coffee. It'll save me from going down into the kitchen.

LA FICELLE: Coffee! Right away! There it is!

---

[3] We have kept the characters' colorful nicknames in the original French, but have provided an approximate translation in the cast list on page 15.

(*The servant leans down and picks up a tray with a coffee service.*)

SERVANT: Thanks, muck snipe!

LA FICELLE: Hey! Try showing some respect, flunkey!

(*The servant places the coffee on a table in the garden. Meanwhile, the Marquis and Marquise du Touchais, their son, Maxime, followed by Monsieur Bourrelier and his daughter, Cécily, come out of the French doors and walk down from the terrace to the garden.*)

BOURRELIER: Marquis, I don't know how to thank you for such wonderful hospitality!

MARQUIS: Isn't it quite natural, my dear Monsieur Bourrelier, that, since you surprised us by visiting us in the afternoon with your lovely daughter, that we would insist on keeping you for dinner?

BOURRELIER: I apologize for forcing you to have dinner so early, Marquis, but it is absolutely necessary that I get back to Dieppe this very evening. I have an important meeting with one of my agents. I'm actually a bit taken up with my own affairs at the moment.

MARQUIS: My dear chap, that's what it means to be the largest ship-owner in the region.

CÉCILY: (*passing the coffee with Maxime's assistance*) One lump or two?

MARQUISE: Two please, my little Cécily. It becomes you nicely to play the young lady of the house.

MARQUIS: Isn't she every day?

BOURRELIER: (*to Maxime*) And what are you doing at the moment, young man? Any hobbies?

MAXIME: During the day, I play golf, cricket and tennis; in the evening, cards and tango.

BOURRELIER: That's frightening! I see why you seem a bit tired. Wouldn't you prefer to spend your time in more profitable ways?

MAXIME: For the moment, things are going very well the way they are.

MARQUIS: My son is joking. He's not taking enough credit for the sheer amount of work that he does and which sometimes weighs too heavily on him.

MARQUISE: (*to Cécily*) My dear child, would you come and walk with me in the park now that the heat has died down?

CÉCILY: Very willingly, Madame!

MARQUISE: (*to Maxime*) Maxime, give me your arm.

(*The Marquise leaves by the rear accompanied by Maxime and Cécily. The Marquis and Bourrelier have liqueurs and cigars.*)

MARQUIS: Well, my dear friend, can you now give me your answer to my proposal?

BOURRELIER: What proposal would that be, my dear Marquis?

MARQUIS: You know very well: the marriage of our two children.

BOURRELIER: Ah yes. I've thought about it for a long while. My first concern, of course, is to guarantee my daughter's happiness.

MARQUIS: Maxime is ready to assume a very respectable position in society. He is, after all, the heir to a great name.

BOURRELIER: But you are ruined, my dear Marquis.

MARQUIS: Let's not exaggerate. Our fortune may not be what it once was, but we're still quite comfortable.

BOURRELIER: Let's be honest, shall we? You have gambled away your wife's fortune on unlucky speculations. Your lands are mortgaged to the hilt, and so is your chateau, from its cellar to its attic. All because of your mismanagement and taste for excessive spending. In short, you have reduced your wife's fortune to nothing.

MARQUIS: You're hard on me, Monsieur Bourrelier.

BOURRELIER: I'm a businessman, first and foremost, and I do not trouble myself with vain sentimentality. Besides, it's not your lack of money that makes me uneasy. My Cécily will have enough for two. Having worked hard all my life to elevate myself, it won't displease me–far from it!–to have my daughter join the Aristocracy. But your son doesn't possess the qualities that would make him a good husband. He is lazy, a gambler, debauched–his reputation is terrible.

MARQUIS: You mustn't say such things. People like to spread gossip; high society can be so nasty. Indeed, I've heard it said that you, yourself, have engaged into some illicit affair with your daughter's tutor–Jacqueline Mascart...

(*Bourrelier barely represses a guilty gesture.*)

MARQUIS: No need to tell you that I don't believe a word of it. So I beg you to extend the same courtesy to my son. I see only good coming out from the merging of our families. The Touchais coat-of-arms emblazoned on the flag of your ships would give them a certain allure. What do you think?

BOURRELIER: It's very tempting, I concede.

MARQUIS: Maxime can be a bit frivolous, overly generous perhaps...

BOURRELIER: Well, I suppose that's a sign of good breeding...

MARQUIS: ...But he has a great deal of heart and will make your daughter very happy. Do we have a deal?

BOURRELIER: In principle, yes, but I still have to talk to Cécily about it.

(*At this moment, Cécily enters from the rear, heading toward the terrace.*)

MARQUIS: Here she is. Now is the time.

BOURRELIER: You're in such a hurry!

MARQUIS: Isn't it better to get it settled?

BOURRELIER: Cécily, what happened to Madame la Marquise?

CÉCILY: I've come back to collect her scarf.

MARQUIS: My son could have spared you that task, my dear.

CÉCILY: Maxime went to telephone his friend, Monsieur de Pont-Marie.

BOURRELIER: I want to talk to you, child.

CÉCILY: But the Marquise is waiting for her scarf.

MARQUIS: I'll take care of it.

(*He finds the scarf and leaves.*)

BOURRELIER: My child, I have to inform you of a marriage proposal that I have just received on your behalf, and which I must answer promptly.

CÉCILY: Is it from Maxime du Touchais?

BOURRELIER: Yes.

CÉCILY: I refuse!

BOURRELIER: Now, Cécily, you're no longer a child, so no caprices. Maxime is a very advantageous match. I beg you to consider his proposal seriously because it deserves attention.

CÉCILY: Father, I told you already: I refuse.

BOURRELIER: At least, give me a reason why.

CÉCILY: It's very simple. My heart's already taken.

BOURRELIER: What! You love someone and you never told me! You know that I'm the best and the weakest of fathers. I would have no prejudices against anyone you'd select. I just want to know who he is.

CÉCILY: It's my cousin, Marcel Garavan.

BOURRELIER: (*stupefied*) Marcel Garavan! But he works for me!

CÉCILY: So what? I don't see that as a dishonor!

BOURRELIER: You must be joking!

CÉCILY: Not at all! If I can't marry him, I won't marry anyone else.

BOURRELIER: So I would have worked hard to build my fortune just to give my daughter, my sole heir, to one of my salesmen–to a Garavan!

CÉCILY: He's your sister's son.

BOURRELIER: All the more reason! When one doesn't go up in the world, one is going down. I could make you a Marquise, and you tell me that you prefer to become Madame Garavan. It's laughable.

CÉCILY: I don't think so! Far from the multitude of suitors who are attracted to me like flies to honey, I have discovered the one man who, terrified by your millions, would be content to live in my shadow and love me in silence, without daring to raise his eyes to me. I know the exquisite sensation of being loved for myself alone, without inappropriate calculations of interest, and you want me to relinquish this happiness? Absolutely not, father! Marcel Garavan is a straight, honest and simple heart, who, at least, knew how to not engage in promiscuous liaisons. Instead, who is the husband you are offering me? A tired nobleman who would bring, along with the deficiencies of his ancestors, those that are the result of his life of debauchery and sloth.

BOURRELIER: It was never my intention to impose Maxime du Touchais on you, but as regards your cousin, never, you hear me! Never will I consent to it! And to cut this ridiculous idyll short, I will order him to leave on my first steamer.

CÉCILY: Your action will be quite useless, because when you love the way Marcel and I love each other, distance doesn't matter.

BOURRELIER: We'll see about that!

(*Seeing the Marquis, his wife and Maxime entering from the left, Bourrelier heads towards them.*)

BOURRELIER: We are going to take our leave after all, Marquis. I sincerely apologize, but time is passing and I can't take a chance on missing my meeting in Dieppe.

MARQUISE: In that case, please leave Cécily with us, my dear Bourrelier–if she won't be too bored. It's still early, and you could come and get her when you return.

BOURRELIER: If my daughter consents, why not?

MARQUIS: (*aside to Bourrelier*) Well? What is the result of your conversation?

BOURRELIER: (*aside to the Marquis*) My daughter is a child who won't be pushed; leave it to me; things will go better that way. (*to the Marquise*) My respects, Madame la Marquise. I'll take the train; I'll arrive faster.

MARQUIS: Are you leaving on foot, my dear friend?

BOURRELIER: After such a fine dinner, the walk will do me good. Dieppe is not so far from Puys. I'll take the cliff-side road.

(*Bourrelier leaves.*)

MARQUISE: (*to Cécily*) If you'd like, Cécily, we could wait in the salon. (*calling*) Reine!

(*Reine, a lady companion of about fifty, appears on the terrace*)

MARQUISE: Would you set the gaming table?

REINE: Of course, Madame.

(*She goes into the chateau by one of the French doors.*)

MARQUISE: I am going to beat you at cards, my little friend. It's an old lady's privilege. You get better at cards as your hair gets whiter.

(*The Marquise and Cécily climb the stairs and leave by one of the French doors. Maxime is about to follow them.*)

MARQUIS: (*to Maxime.*) One moment, Maxime.

(*Maxime turns toward his father.*)

MARQUIS: You seem to be forcing yourself to be in a good mood today. What's bothering you?

MAXIME: Nothing, father. I'm waiting for George, that's all.

MARQUIS: You and your friend George de Pont-Marie are most likely blundering badly into some kind of shady business, I suspect.

MAXIME: No, not at all, father, I assure you.

MARQUIS: Whatever may be the case, I advise you, in your own interest, to watch your conduct. At the moment, I am focusing all my efforts to make you an acceptable fiancé for Cécily Bourrelier, but, I beg you, do take a little care of your reputation–it is deplorable.

MAXIME: I understand, father. If you see me so preoccupied, it's because I absolutely need a sum of money–oh! a mere trifle–200 francs. Could you loan them to me?

MARQUIS: I don't have it.

MAXIME: But only this morning, you received several rents?

MARQUIS: And tomorrow, I have many bills due, which makes it completely impossible for me to spare a *centime*. No use insisting. When I can do it, I do it, but today, I cannot.

(*The Marquis leaves by the terrace. At this moment, George de Pont-Marie enters wearing a grey colored felt hat.*)

MAXIME: (*going quickly to de Pont-Marie*) Did you succeed?

PONT-MARIE: No. That's why I'm so late. No one wants to lend us any money any more. Did you ask your father?

MAXIME: He's obstinately refusing, under the pretence that he needs his money to pay his bills.

PONT-MARIE: What to do? In your set, you see no one else? (*a pause*) What about Bourrelier, rumored to be your future father-in-law?

MAXIME: He won't advance me a *sou*.

PONT-MARIE: How do you know?

MAXIME: I'm sure of it. He doesn't like me.

PONT-MARIE: You can still try...

MAXIME: Time's wasting! If I don't pay tomorrow, I'll be banned from the club.

PONT-MARIE: What about me? I might be prosecuted for fraud. Go on, let's ask him! Let's go to his villa. If you like, I'll come with you.

MAXIME: He dined here and just left for Dieppe, but he's got to return to collect his daughter.

PONT-MARIE: Let's meet him on the way then.

MAXIME: He went on foot, on the cliff-side road. He'll certainly return the same way...

PONT-MARIE: (*edgy*) You're sure of that?

MAXIME: Why?

PONT-MARIE: (*after a pause*) For no reason. (*abruptly*) Let's not waste ant more time. We must have the money this evening, no matter what it takes. Come on, let's go.

(*They leave hurriedly by the side. A moment passes, then Chéri-Bibi enters from the side. He is dressed very simply. He looks around, then heads rapidly toward the kitchen window and calls.*)

CHÉRI-BIBI: Hey! La Ficelle! It is I, Chéri-Bibi!

LA FICELLE: (*inside*) Wait–I'm coming!

(*La Ficelle appears, dressed as a scullery boy, first in the window frame, then enters.*)

LA FICELLE: I'm happy to see you. (*shaking Chéri-Bibi's hand*) Your shift is already over?

CHÉRI-BIBI: No, but I left the shop anyway. Tomorrow, I'm going away. I asked the boss for a day off to accompany Jacqueline to the convent. You know that my poor little sister is taking the veil?

LA FICELLE: Ah, yes. After what happened with Bourrelier...

CHÉRI-BIBI: That wretch! To attack a poor defenseless child like that... Ruin her honor... But Jacqueline was determined to see Mademoiselle Cécily one last time before taking the veil. It's not the daughter's fault, after all, if the father is a scumbag. But, as I didn't want my sister going to the villa, on account of Bourrelier, and as I learned in the village that they were dining here tonight, I brought Jacqueline here. She's waiting at the gamekeeper's house.

LA FICELLE: And also, admit it, you'll be pleased to see Mademoiselle Cécily.

CHÉRI-BIBI: Yes, La Ficelle, it causes me great joy and great pain at the same time. You recall that, when we were kids, we all played together. She wasn't Mademoiselle Bourrelier then. There was no difference between us; she was just a kid, like us. Seeing her every day, I began to love her a little. But the years went by, and as they did, the barrier that separated us became unbreakable. Alas, the heart don't accommodate itself of social differences. I haven't stopped loving her, but because she is now very rich, it's without hope. Still, I love her, La Ficelle, and I'm really miserable.

LA FICELLE: Look, Chéri-Bibi, you're not being reasonable. You know that a love like that is impossible. Where will it lead you?

CHÉRI-BIBI: I'm not even thinking of that; it's of her alone that I think.

LA FICELLE: Poor Chéri-Bibi! And as for me, I'd like to see you happy! I would give up my life to guarantee your happiness, as you risked yours to save me that day on the beach when the riptide was carrying me away.

CHÉRI-BIBI: I'd have done better to die myself that day; at least, I wouldn't have to endure all the tortures that are tearing me apart now. And the one I adore would have to be the daughter of the man who seduced my poor Jacqueline. Ah! Misfortune!

(*Cécily appears on the terrace in the moonlight seemingly looking for someone.*)

CHÉRI-BIBI: Here she is! (*he remains ecstatic.*)

LA FICELLE: (*to Chéri-Bibi*) Go and speak to her!

CHÉRI-BIBI: No. Let me stay in the shadows. That's the story of my love, you see.

LA FICELLE: My word, you're terrible at this! (*calling softly*) Mademoiselle Cécily!

CÉCILY: Is that you, La Ficelle? You haven't seen my father return?

LA FICELLE: No, Mademoiselle. But there's someone here who's like to speak to you. Jean Mascart, you remember him? Chéri-Bibi?

CÉCILY: I'm coming down.

(*She rapidly descends the stairway.*)

CÉCILY: Good evening, Jean.

CHÉRI-BIBI: (*hardly able to open his mouth*) Good evening, Mademoiselle Cécily.

CÉCILY: (*offering her hand*) Why, you aren't offering me your hand!

CHÉRI-BIBI: (*very embarrassed*) I don't dare (*taking her hand, still embarrassed*) My sister Jacqueline is here. She would be happy to see you, because, tomorrow, you know, she's going to join the nuns of Saint Vincent de Paul.

CÉCILY: I plan to be there at the ceremony when she takes the veil. But I'd be delighted to see her this evening.

CHÉRI-BIBI: In that case, I'll go and get her.

(*Chéri-Bibi leaves by the side.*)

CÉCILY: (*to La Ficelle*) I'm surprised that my father hasn't returned yet. Would you be kind enough to go and look for him at the entrance of the park?

LA FICELLE: My pleasure, Mademoiselle Cécily!

(*He leaves. Then, Jacqueline enters, escorted by Chéri-Bibi.*)

CÉCILY: My little Jacqueline! (*they embrace*)

CHÉRI-BIBI: I'll wait for you here, little sister.

CÉCILY: Don't bother. Since my father is late, I'll go into the villa with Jacqueline. Reine will accompany us. Then, I'll send Jacqueline home.

CHÉRI-BIBI: (*with regret*) I see. So I'll be going then... (*bowing to Cécily*) Mademoiselle.

(*He leaves.*)

CÉCILY: So, Jacqueline, your decision is irrevocable?

JACQUELINE: Yes, Mademoiselle. Tomorrow, I will be a nun.

CÉCILY: You were my tutor; you were bright and happy. Then, there were these few weeks when you left our house under the pretext of health. And when you returned, you said you planned to enter a convent. Your vocation came to you so suddenly?

JACQUELINE: Er, yes. Circumstances caused it to develop spontaneously.

CÉCILY: You are really going to say good-bye to the world?

JACQUELINE: Without any regrets. The ugliness I've suffered was enough to separate me from it forever.

CÉCILY: It takes courage to leave it.

JACQUELINE: It takes an even greater deal of courage to stay in it. I'm not complaining, Mademoiselle Cécily. Instead of sadness, I will find peace and rest. I will raise children, I will care for the sick, and the days of my life will shine like the beads of a rosary.

CÉCILY: You were like a sister to me, Jacqueline, kiss me.

(*Reine appears on the terrace and comes down the stairs.*)

REINE: You forgot your cloak, Mademoiselle Cécily. It's cold tonight.

(*She gives Cécily a cloak with a Capuchin's hood.*)

CÉCILY: Jacqueline is with me. Will you take her home later?

REINE: Of course!

CÉCILY: (*to Jacqueline*) Then, come, Jacqueline. I want you to remember forever the last night you spent in the world with me.

(*Cécily and Jacqueline leave, followed by Reine. A moment passes, then de Pont-Marie is seen entering furtively by the rear. He makes sure he cannot be seen, then furtively climbs the stairway and goes into the chateau by one of the French doors. Unseen by him, Chéri-Bibi has spotted him and follows him inside. Soon thereafter, we hear a violent brouhaha and Costaud enters, followed by several police officers and peasants carrying torches.*)

COSTAUD: (*to a servant*) Inform Monsieur le Marquis du Touchais that Sergeant Costaud from the Dieppe Police wishes to speak to him immediately.

(*As the servant starts up the stairway shouting and calling, Maxime enters suddenly by one of the French doors, holding Chéri-Bibi by the collar.*)

MAXIME: Help! I've just found my father struck dead in his office next to his safe. (*a pause.*) It can only be the work of this wretch! (*pointing to Chéri-Bibi*)

COSTAUD: What a terrible development! And I had just come to inform Monsieur le Marquis that Monsieur Bourrelier has just been found murdered on the cliffs

(*Chéri-Bibi remains speechless.*)

COSTAUD: (*to Chéri-Bibi*) Answer my questions. What were you doing at the chateau at this hour?

CHÉRI-BIBI: I am innocent!

COSTAUD: Answer!

CHERI BIBI: (*gripped by a violent emotion*) I was returning to Dieppe by the cliff-side road when I saw two men fighting. One of them might have been Monsieur Bourrelier. I couldn't distinguish the features of the other man, because his face was hidden by a grey hat. Suddenly, Monsieur Bourrelier was pushed violently and fell off the edge of the cliff. The man in the grey hat fled. I followed him. He entered the chateau, I entered after him.

Then, I found myself in complete darkness. Suddenly (*pointing to Maxime*), Monsieur Maxime sprang up and grabbed me. That's the whole truth, I swear!

COSTAUD: So the author of these two crimes would be a man in a grey hat! What kind of fancy story is this? (*to the policemen*) Officers, search the house, just in case.

(*Two officers enter the chateau.*)

COSTAUD: (*to Chéri-Bibi*) No doubt, the judge will appreciate your effort of imagination, but it would be much simpler to confess. The first crime, at least, is marvelously clear. It is public notoriety that Monsieur Bourrelier had abused your sister Jacqueline. Revenge would, therefore, be the motive...

CHÉRI-BIBI: But, Sergeant, I swear to you that I'm innocent! The idea that you could mistake me for a murderer is driving me mad.

(*The two officers return.*)

POLICE OFFICER: We didn't find anyone, Sergeant.

COSTAUD: I expected that. Officers, place Jean Mascart, alias Chéri-Bibi, under arrest.

CURTAIN

SCENE II
SISTER MARY OF THE ANGELS

The steamship Bayard. *The stage is made up of three levels offering a cut-through view of the ship:*

The top level is that of the bridge, rising two meters above the main deck. The bridge is connected to the deck by a ladder. On it is a machine gun, pointing at the deck. There is also the wheel-house and, above it, the smoke stacks.

The middle level is that of the main deck, with netting on both sides, ropes and tackle, and a door leading to the lower deck.

Beneath that, the bottom level is that of the lower deck. This one features, center stage, a door with iron bars, which can be closed with a wooden shutter, and a door leading to the upper deck. We can see and hear the ocean through the portholes.

AT RISE, Lieutenant de Vilène, sextant in hand, stands on the bridge plotting the course of the ship. A sailor mounts guard by the machine gun. Captain Barrachon enters the top deck from the door connecting the two decks.

BARRACHON: Have you plotted our course, Lieutenant?

DE VILENE: Yes, Captain. We are 32 degrees, 20 minutes, latitude North and 24 degrees, 50 minutes, longitude West, from the Paris meridian.

BARRACHON: Good man. Can you come down a moment? I have something to tell you.

DE VILENE: Aye, aye, Captain.

(*He comes down the ladder.*)

BARRACHON: (*confidentially*) I've just seen him in his cell...

DE VILENE: Is he in a better mood?

BARRACHON: Quite the opposite...

DE VILENE: And yet, the manacles always brings reason even to the most bull-headed of convicts.

BARRACHON: My dear de Vilène, that bull-headed man is the worst prisoner I've ever seen since I've been commanding the *Bayard* and transporting convicts to their penal servitude.

DE VILENE: He's been rendered completely powerless. He's better off behind the bars of his cell, that in the middle of his comrades.

BARRACHON: Do you know what he said to me when I asked him why he spat in my face?

DE VILENE: Which was the cause of all the stern measures taken against him.

BARRACHON: He said: "You were wrong to take it as a personal insult. Consider instead that I was spitting in the face of society."

DE VILENE: The wretch! Luckily for all of us, he'll die before the end of the journey. His feet and hands were already bloody this morning.

BARRACHON: (*considering*) The Devil! Now there's a matter of conscience...

DE VILENE: Should your conscience torment you when it comes to men like him? They're unredeemable–they'll always be pigs!

BARRACHON: I've never been more in a hurry to reach Cayenne.

DE VILENE: Then, what are you worried about, Captain?

BARRACHON: Nothing. But I'll admit to you that this Chéri-Bibi keeps me awake at night.

DE VILENE: Why, Good Lord! He's a vulgar criminal, who, but for the ridiculous sentimentality of the jury, ought to have been guillotined mercilessly.

BARRACHON: He's a repeat offender. He's already escaped from prison.

DE VILENE: Once is not a habit. His cage, with steel bars 30 millimeters in diameter, shackles and padlocks, will not so easily give up its prey.

BARRACHON: At least, make sure that two guards never take their eyes off him.

DE VILENE: Worry no more about Chéri-Bibi, Captain. You're really doing him too much honor!

(*The Chief Guard, Pascaud, enters, followed by a sailor carrying a bell that rings twice.*)

DE VILENE: Ah. It's time for the stroll of the convicts.

BARRACHON: (*calling the Chief*) Pascaud!

PASCAUD: Yes Captain?

BARRACHON: You will give the order to rotate the guards watching Chéri-Bibi every hour. That will be less exhausting. You know the password. Don't ever say it aloud, and never speak to Prisoner No. 3216.

PASCAUD: Yes, Captain.

BARRACHON: (*to de Vilène*) Walk with me, Lieutenant. We're going to go through the lower deck and inspect the cages in detail. All the cages. I've got a feeling that something unusual is going to happen...

(*Followed by de Vilène, Barrachon walks through the door leading down to the lower deck. Pascaud then opens the wooden shutters, revealing the metal cages in which the convicts are kept. Some pass their hands through the bars.*)

PASCAUD: Let's go–convicts on deck!

(*Gueule-de-Bois, Petit-Bon-Dieu, Le Rouquin, Le Kanak and other convicts emerge from the cages, carefully watched by the guards, revolvers drawn. The prisoners' faces are filled with despair. They all wear uniforms with their respective numbers printed on their hats.*)

GUARD: (*pushing them*) Try to hurry up! What a bunch of malingerers.

LE ROUQUIN: No need to shove me.

GUARD: What? The gentleman demands respect!

LE ROUQUIN: Ah! If we ever meet again face to face...

PASCAUD: (*to the convicts*) I don't want to hear any noise during the stroll, understood? The first one caught gabbing will join Chéri-Bibi in his private cabin, or will get acquainted with this. (*pointing to his revolver*)

GUEULE-DE-BOIS: (*to Petit-Bon-Dieu*) All the same, it's better to be here than below, where the guards beat us. (*pointing to the guards out of the corner of his eye*) What do you think, Petit-Bon-Dieu?

PETIT-BON-DIEU: I think the same as you, friend Gueule-de-Bois. As long as the sea is a bit rough this morning, some of our chums would enjoy giving the fish something to eat! Don't tell me that it wouldn't be fun.

LE ROUQUIN: (*joining in*) We sure could use some fun!

PETIT-BON-DIEU: You said it! Rouquin, my dream has always been to become a honest man.

GUEULE-DE-BOIS: Why?

PETIT-BON-DIEU: To set myself up as a wine merchant.

LE ROUQUIN: Get out! What an ambitious little guy!

GUEULE-DE-BOIS: Hey! Not everybody can be a wine merchant. That would be too easy. Each man's destiny has already been written when he comes into the world. Thus, you, Petit-Bon-Dieu, were destined to chop wood in Cayenne. As Chéri-Bibi says: What's written is written. Fatality!

PETIT-BON-DIEU: Pfft! That's just stories to frighten children! (*lowering his voice*) The moment has come to speak seriously. Look, is it for today or for tomorrow?

LE ROUQUIN: (*loudly*) Yes. Is it for today or for to-morrow?

GUEULE-DE-BOIS: Your voice! Christ! Speak lower!

PASCAUD: (*from the bridge*) I thought just now I had impressed upon you the necessity for absolute silence! (*pointing to his revolver*) Must I provide you with more convincing arguments?

LE ROUQUIN: (*between his teeth*) Ah! The brutes!

GUEULE-DE-BOIS: I would give my share of beans to get my paws on one of 'em!

(*Pascaud and the guards resume talking.*)

PETIT-BON-DIEU: (*whispering*) Then things are going to get hot?

GUEULE-DE-BOIS: For some; and it's not going to be put off any longer.

LE KANAK: (*who has been part of the group from the beginning but has remained silent*) Going to be some trouble. I don't like trouble.

GUEULE-DE-BOIS: (*guffawing*) Oh! Kanak! Suck on it! Trouble makes you queasy now, eh? Did you feel that way when you were cutting up your patients and using strips of their flesh to amuse yourself?

LE KANAK: (*angry*) Shut up!

GUEULE-DE-BOIS: You shut up, you cannibal!

PETIT-BON-DIEU: Shut both your mouths! We've got better things to do than reviewing each other's youthful peccadilloes!

GUEULE-DE-BOIS: Yes! We must follow the orders of our leader, Chéri-Bibi, because he is superior to us in every respect.

LE ROUQUIN: Even though, he began his criminal career by being innocent.

PETIT-BON-DIEU: (*pretentiously*) And I'm using his case as an example in the book I'm writing on the reform of our judicial system.

LE KANAK: Poet!

PETIT-BON-DIEU: Ah, it's not learning that I lack!

LE ROUQUIN: But now you want to become a wine merchant!

PETIT-BON-DIEU: The legal profession disgusts me. During my, er, nervous breakdowns, I've stabbed 18 lawyers and one solicitor who refused to give me the key to his strong box.

LE ROUQUIN: That's the way things are in this world. It's enough to be innocent to be thrown in jail. I've only stabbed five people–my word of honor!–Not one more, not one less. Well, it's for a sixth stiff, whom I'd never even met, that you have the pleasure of my company.

LA KANAK: (*smirking*) Another judicial error!

PETIT-BON-DIEU: And meanwhile, our poor Chéri-Bibi is in chains.

GUEULE-DE-BOIS: And I have the notion that they put him there for some good reasons.

LA ROUQUIN: So I ask again: is it for today or for tomorrow?

GUEULE-DE-BOIS: (*emphasizing his words*) It's for when Chéri-Bibi says it is.

ALL: (*singing together in chorus*) The Republic screws us. / From Boulogne to Pantruches / Who makes things go tick-tock? / It's Chéri-Bibi!

PASCAUD: (*on the bridge, hopping mad*) You scum! You dare screw with me!

(*Followed by some guards, he runs down the ladder and lines up the convicts by force, elbowing and pushing them.*)

PASCAUD: I want a straight line. More! Straighter! More!

(*Lieutenant de Vilène enters by the door leading to the lower deck.*)

DE VILENE: They won't be calm, unless they're deprived of food. That'll teach them not to sing. They must be delighted that their friend Chéri-Bibi is in the lock-up!

(*La Ficelle, dressed as a scullion, enters from the hold, dragging buckets containing food for the convicts.*)

PASCAUD: (*to La Ficelle*) What are you waiting for to give them their grub?

LA FICELLE: (*frightened*) I don't dare come forward.

DE VILENE: It's obvious you're afraid, my lad.

LA FICELLE: Lieutenant, I am frightfully afraid of these (*hesitating*) gentlemen.

PASCAUD: (*bursting into laughter*) These gentlemen! That's a good one!

(*All the guards burst into laughter.*)

DE VILENE: With cold feet like that, you shouldn't have signed on the *Bayard*. Start serving the food. (*to the convicts*) But before you eat, listen up. I've just inspected your cages. They're filthy. The men on fatigue duty will stay on duty for another 24 hours, and will not be authorized to follow the others on deck during the daily stroll until after their work is done. I want your cages to be as clean as the Captain's quarters. Do you understand, Le Rouquin?

LE ROUQUIN: But the Captain said...

DE VILENE: (*putting his revolver right under Le Rouquin's nose*) As far as you're concerned, this is the only Captain aboard!

(*The guards burst out laughing again.*)

DE VILENE: Enough! (*to La Ficelle*) Take back some of the food. Two buckets will do, since they're not well behaved.

(*La Ficelle returns back to the lower deck with all but two of his buckets. Another Guard enters from the door.*)

GUARD: Lieutenant, the Countess is requesting insistently to talk to you.

DE VILENE: What does she want?

GUARD: I don't know. She says that it is to you alone she must speak.

DE VILENE: (*after having considered*) Very well. Bring her to me.

(*A moment goes by, then the Countess enters, escorted by the guard. She's a woman of rare beauty. She wears the uniform of a convict.*)

DE VILENE: You asked to speak to me alone?

COUNTESS: Alone or in public, it's all the same to me. For a long time, I've had a mad desire to pull your beard, and I'm going to satisfy it. (*rushing at him like a fury*) I've got him by the beard! I've got him by the beard!

ALL THE CONVICTS: Go for it, Countess!

(*The guards hurl themselves on the Countess and, with blows from their revolver butts free, the Lieutenant.*)

DE VILENE: Put this woman in irons immediately!

(*Two guards drag the Countess away.*)

DE VILENE: (*to the convicts*) As for you lot, I'm hereby authorizing the guards to shoot the first one of you who budges. (*to Pascaud*) Come, Pascaud, let's go down to the lower deck.

(*He goes out, followed by Pascaud.*)

GUARD: Fall out!

(*The convicts, gesticulating wildly, jostling each other, hurl themselves like starving animals on the two buckets of food.*)

GUEULE-DE-BOIS: Hey! Watch out!

LE ROUQUIN: You were going to spill some beans on the deck.

PETIT-BON-DIEU: This isn't bad grub!

(*Petit-Bon-Dieu, Le Kanak, Gueule-de-Bois and Le Rouquin eat in silence around the same bucket.*)

LE ROUQUIN: (*to Le Kanak*) Say, Kanak, why does your crazy mistress, the Countess, wants to pull the Lieutenant's beard?

LE KANAK: (*mysteriously*) It's her nerves.

PETIT-BON-DIEU: Women are such complicated creatures! Especially the Countess... Didn't she help you operate on your patients, Kanak?

LE KANAK: Enough! I've already told you, I don't like anyone to speak to me about that.

PETIT-BON-DIEU: OK! I'll shut my trap.

LE ROUQUIN: (*as he eats*) It's not criticize the Republic, but they could spend a little more food-wise. That grub's nothing like that famous Spanish cod that Chéri-Bibi keeps telling us about.

GUEULE-DE-BOIS: At the Santé prison, where I made my debut, the food was better.

PETIT-BON-DIEU: As for me, I used to go to Vichy every year to take the waters.

LE ROUQUIN: Say, pals, if we get to be the masters of this ship, what will we do next?

PETIT-BON-DIEU: Well, we could become pirates. (*to Gueule-de-Bois*) Not so, my little friend?

LE KANAK: We'd be kings of the ocean.

GUEULE-DE-BOIS: Hey! Look sharp! (*pointing to a guard heading towards them*) A screw!

PETIT-BON-DIEU: Let's sing so he won't know what we're talking about.

(*They sing–the guard passes by.*)

GUEULE-DE-BOIS: Might be nice to go where there's a revolution. We could offer our services to the revolutionary army. Better still, we could even become the government!

PETIT-BON-DIEU: That's a wonderful idea! You could be minister of justice, and I would be minister of education. You'd see how well I'd educate people. There will no longer be any need for assassins!

LE KANAK: (*coldly*) And now that you've shared your delusions with us, Gueule-de-Bois, maybe you might tell us how, without weapons, locked in cages, and surrounded by guards, ever ready to whip us, we might take over the *Bayard*?

GUEULE-DE-BOIS: The Doctor is curious! (*low and quickly*) Chéri-Bibi said we'll have enough weapons to render us masters of the lower deck. When the time comes, we'll hurl ourselves on those we find there and kill them all.

LE KANAK: But the guards will fire! We're the ones who'll be massacred!

GUEULE-DE-BOIS: Trust me! They'll barely have time to move. More than one of them will bite the dust. The thing is not to be scared, and run as fast as possible. So much the worse for cowards! As for me, I prefer to croak like that, than die slowly in Cayenne chopping wood.

LE KANAK: I still want proof that we will have weapons, just as Chéri-Bibi said we would.

GUEULE-DE-BOIS: Proof! Proof! We have enough balls that we don't need it! But I'll show you. Rouquin, look in your bag. (*gesturing*)

LE ROUQUIN: (*searching his bag*) What's that I feel?

GUEULE-DE-BOIS: Hurry up!

(*Suddenly, Le Rouquin pulls a bottle of rum from his bag.*)

LE ROUQUIN: How's that possible?

PETIT-BON-DIEU: A bottle of rum! A real one!

GUEULE-DE-BOIS: You see, Kanak: just as Chéri-Bibi sends us rum, when he wants to, he'll send us guns.

(*The convicts extend their hands to grasp the bottle.*)

GUEULE-DE-BOIS: Put your paws down! Take your numbers, like at the lottery. (*to Kanak*) And since you're the who required proof, you'll drink after the pals. I begin.

(*He takes the bottle and pours its contents down his throat without touching his lips.*)

LE ROUQUIN: Not so fast. Leave some...

PETIT-BON-DIEU: You're going to get the hiccups.

(*Suddenly, Captain Barrachon returns from the lower decks at the head of some guards and sailors.*)

LE KANAK: We're done for!

(*The convicts remain glued to the spot.*)

BARRACHON: (*to Gueule-de-Bois*) What's that you've got there? Rum?

(*Gueule-de-Bois is struck dumb.*)

BARRACHON: Booze in the hands of convicts. It's unimaginable! (*to Pascaud*) Find out what happened at once! If a guard is at fault, punish him severely!

(*Pascaud leaves just as Lieutenant de Vilène enters, looking very upset.*)

DE VILENE: Captain!

BARRACHON: What?

(*De Vilène pulls Barrachon aside.*)

DE VILENE: No. 3216 has escaped!

BARRACHON: Chéri-Bibi!

DE VILENE: Yes, Captain Chéri-Bibi is no longer in his cell.

BARRACHON: (*staggering*) That's impossible. (*to the guards*) Lock up all the convicts immediately! And put a guard in front of every cage.

GUEULE-DE-BOIS: (*to Petit-Bon-Dieu*) Looks like something's going on.

(*The guards quickly push the convicts through the doors to the cages and leave with them.*)

BARRACHON: What about the two guards that were guarding him? What happened to them?

DE VILENE: They're dead. The relief guard was just found strangled behind the cell door. The irons are still locked. But Chéri-Bibi is gone. He's vanished.

BARRACHON: (*panicked*) We must search the ship!

DE VILENE: Yes, but we must conceal his escape. The convicts are plotting something, I'm sure of it, and Chéri-Bibi's disappearance might trigger a full-blown revolt. Also, the personnel on board are terrified of Chéri-Bibi. If they find out he's escaped...

BARRACHON: You're right.

(*Pascaud returns, looking frightened.*)

PASCAUD: Captain! Have you heard?...

BARRACHON: Yes, Pascaud. Chéri-Bibi has escaped.

PASCAUD: Not only Chéri-Bibi, Captain, but also the Countess, who was in a neighboring cell.. She's escaped as well.

(*Barrachon and de Vilène are both stunned.*)

BARRACHON/DE VILENE: The Countess, too!

PASCAUD: Yes, Captain. Her cell is empty.

BARRACHON: Listen, Pascaud, you know I do trust you, but is it possible that, perhaps, you turned a blind eye...?

PASCAUD: No, Captain! I haven't left the deck. My men can tell you. Also, I couldn't spring Chéri-Bibi, even if I wanted to, because I don't have the key to his chains. And do you think I could have murdered two of my fellow guards?

DE VILENE: The Captain isn't accusing you, Pascaud. He's searching for answers. No one knows where Chéri-Bibi is.

PASCAUD: He's got to be on board somewhere. But what's even scarier is that the others in their cages suspect something. They were waiting for something like this to happen. My word.

DE VILENE: The fact is, they've been up to something for the last two days.

BARRACHON: Above all, we must keep our heads. What do you recommend, Lieutenant?

DE VILENE: First of all, Pascaud is going to spread the rumor that Chéri-Bibi's dead. Then, if you agree, Captain, we should search the ship from top to bottom. We cannot not find them, and when we do, we'll make them run the gauntlet.

BARRACHON: I approve. (*to Pascaud*) Execute the Lieutenant's order, Pascaud.

(*Pascaud leaves after having given a military salute.*)

BARRACHON: Between the two of us, Lieutenant, I still believe that there must be some accomplice on board. Nothing else can explain Chéri-Bibi's escape.

DE VILENE: I agree, Captain, but not among the guards. I'm thinking of the women being transported... Did you notice how beautiful the Kanak's mistress, the one they call the Countess, is?...

BARRACHON: I see. You think that she might have seduced one of the sailors...

(*La Ficelle enters from the lower deck, running crazily.*)

LA FICELLE: I saw him! I saw him!

(*He bumps into the Captain.*)

BARRACHON: What is it, man?

LA FICELLE: Help! Help! Chéri-Bibi's on the loose! Chéri-Bibi's escaped!

DE VILENE: (*trying to stop him*) Shut up! Will you shut up!

(*But La Ficelle gets loose and runs away screaming.*)

LA FICELLE: Chéri-Bibi's escaped! Chéri-Bibi's escaped!

DE VILENE: The news has already spread!

BARRACHON: It's unimaginable! We're confronted to a painful mystery.

DE VILENE: Trust me, Captain. We must search the ship at once and catch Chéri-Bibi. The sooner the better.

BARRACHON: Right away. Let me issue some new instructions to the night officer, because it's going to be night soon.

(*Indeed, night starts to fall. They head toward the stairway and, as they reach the first steps, a sister of charity enters furtively from the lower decks, casting uneasy glances left and right. She does not see the Captain and the Lieutenant, who are hidden by the ladder, but they see her plainly.*)

DE VILENE: (*to Barrachon*) That's Sister Mary of the Angels. Why has she left the Infirmary? Look, Captain! It's almost as if she's trying to make sure she's alone on the deck.

BARRACHON: Indeed. What strange behavior.

(*She bends forward to drop something taken from inside her large sleeves.*)

DE VILENE: (*low, to Barrachon*) Look, she's slipping a letter between the slats in the deck.

BARRACHON: I will clear this up at once (*calling her*) Sister!

(*He rapidly descends the ladder followed by the Lieutenant. The Sister utters a little scream of surprise and swiftly picks up the letter.*)

SISTER MARY: (*stammering*) What do you want, Captain?

BARRACHON: I want that letter that you just picked up.

SISTER MARY: I didn't–I didn't pick up anything, Captain. I don't know– what you mean...

BARRACHON: Excuse me, Sister, but I hate to hear you commit such a lie. If you don't give me that letter on the spot–a letter the mysterious nature of which clearly warrants my attention –I will call another Sister and have it taken from you by force.

SISTER MARY: (*emotional*) I don't want to–I can't....

DE VILENE: Are you secretly communicating in this way with the convicts? But why?

BARRACHON: (*in a slightly softened voice*) I know what I owe to your character, to the mission you are given down here. But, Sister Mary, understand plainly that there are things which I can't allow. Disobedience mustn't hide behind the mask of charity.

DE VILENE: Sister, why are you being so stubborn?

BARRACHON: You force me to believe that there may be more to this than mere Christian zeal. After all, you've just lied to us! You must have some serious motives for it! Give me that letter!

SISTER MARY: I don't have it! Please, Captain! I beg you to believe me.

(*She falls at the feet of the Captain.*)

BARRACHON: But don't you understand that your attitude makes us imagine the worst? We've been trying to find out how the convicts were able to communicate from cage to cage, from group to group, and form a mysterious conspiracy, the nature of which we ignore. But it presents a threat to us. And now, we discover that it's you who are informing them, and it's you who are informing them! It's you who are their instrument! Oh, God, I do want to believe you, Sister, but for me to do so, I must see that letter.

(*He abruptly grasps her hands and snatches the letter away. She utters a scream and remains annihilated, hands folded in prayer.*)

BARRACHON: (*rapidly unfolding the letter and perusing it rapidly*) "Chéri-Bibi is not dead." Now, this is rather strange! What can Chéri-Bibi have to do with her?

(*Suddenly, we hear the sound of metal being pried loose.*)

DE VILENE: Listen, Captain! It sounds as if someone's trying to force open the gates of his cage. (*pulling his revolver*) We should do something!

BARRACHON: Not yet, Lieutenant. There's still time. Instead, let's continue to observe. I think we're going to witness the solution to our little mystery.

(*The Captain and the Lieutenant climb the ladder. Sister Mary remains on the deck, on her knees, praying. We hear, then see, the shutters on Gueule-de-Bois' cage open–the convict having successfully pried the bolt loose with a very thin metal blade. He now slips furtively onto the deck.*)

GUEULE-DE-BOIS: Decidedly, I haven't lost my touch with locks. I still have it! (*noticing Sister Mary on her knees*) Sister Mary of the Angels!

SISTER MARY: (*rising*) Go away! Go away!

(*De Vilène fires a shot in the air.*)

DE VILENE: (*shouting*) Alert! Alert!

GUEULE-DE-BOIS: Great Scott!

(*Guards surge from the lower deck. Captain Barrachon, followed buy the Lieutenant, leap down from the ladder.*)

BARRACHON: Search this man right away!

DE VILENE: And grab his arms! Quickly!

(*But Gueule-de-Bois knocks two of the guards down, then grabs another by the throat, while taking a piece of paper from his pocket and swallowing it.*)

DE VILENE: He's swallowing a piece of paper!

BARRACHON: (*to the Lieutenant*) Shoot him!

(*The Lieutenant fires his revolver at Gueule-de-Bois just as Sister Mary of the Angels, who has been watching this struggle with anguish, rushes between them. She is the one catching the bullet.*)

ALL: Ah!

(*Sister Mary collapses onto the deck. Gueule-de-Bois Throat is finally overpowered and dragged away by the guards. De Vilène bends down to examine the Nun's wound.*)

DE VILENE: She's wounded in the shoulder.

BARRACHON: (*to one guard*) Go fetch the doctor at once! (*to another*) Take the Sister back to her cabin and post a guard at her door. (*to de Vilène*) Lieutenant, I want you to remain at her bedside. The first words she says, as she wakes up, might doubtlessly be precious to us, understood?

DE VILENE: Perfectly, Captain!

(*He gestures to several sailors to carry Sister Mary who is still in unconscious and leaves with them. In the meantime, night has fallen and it is now dark.*)

BARRACHON: (*striding nervously*) First, Chéri-Bibi and the Countess escape. Then, I find that Sister Mary is somehow involved in all this—yet another new mystery, even more obscure.

(*A trumpet is heard. The Captain heads towards the ladder leading to the bridge when he bumps into a man dressed in a simple sailor's pea-jacket—it is Chéri-Bibi!*)

CHÉRI-BIBI: (*advancing, hand outstretched*) How's it going, Captain?

BARRACHON: (*recoiling*) Who goes there?

CHÉRI-BIBI: Don't you recognize me? (pulling off his pea jacket and beret, revealing his convict uniform, with his number: 3216) It's I, Chéri-Bibi.

BARRACHON: (*terrified*) Chéri-Bibi!

(*The Captain prepares to shout, but Chéri-Bibi points a gun at him.*)

CHÉRI-BIBI: Don't! Be very quiet! Not one shout! Not one gesture! (*pointing to a coil of ropes*) Please be seated. (*insisting*) I beg you.

BARRACHON: Bandit!

CHÉRI-BIBI: No tough talk now, my dear Barrachon. I've been wanting to have a little chat with you for a long time.

BARRACHON: Take care! I won't always be at your mercy.

CHÉRI-BIBI: Let's not speak of the future. (*forcing him to sit*) Sit down, my dear Captain, and let's talk. I am an honest man, Barrachon.

BARRACHON: Let me laugh!

CHÉRI-BIBI: You don't believe me? I was expecting it! Fatality! If only you knew what I've had to endure in life! It isn't to be believed! I will tell you, first of all, that I'm not even angry with my judges over their mistake, because it's human to be deceived. And yet, Captain, the man who is speaking to you right now, and who is inscribed in the register of convicts as No. 3216, is innocent!

BARRACHON: You're not going to tell me that, a few years ago, you did not commit...

CHÉRI-BIBI: Exactly eight years ago.

BARRACHON: ...that double murder near Dieppe, for which you were condemned to forced labor in perpetuity?

CHÉRI-BIBI: I am innocent of those crimes, but that's not what I wanted to discuss with you.

(*A patrol of sailors enters from the lower decks.*)

BARRACHON: A patrol.

(*Chéri-Bibi quickly puts on his pea jacket and sailor cap.*)

CHÉRI-BIBI: Not a word, my dear Captain. You wouldn't want to force me to commit my first crime.

(*Barrachon remains still. The patrol crosses the deck, climbs the ladder and disappears.*)

CHÉRI-BIBI: Excuse me, Captain, for the liberty I am taking in retaining you for a few moments, but I have something to tell you. Returning to Cayenne enrages me! When I escaped from there the first time, I swore never to set foot in that place again. You understand me? If you don't, then we're in for a tricky time.

BARRACHON: I'm not afraid of you.

CHÉRI-BIBI: There are more than 800 men here who will obey me at a glance. You're not strong. They'll make a snack of you.

BARRACHON: And the weapons?

CHÉRI-BIBI: We have them; we will have them. The men are waiting only for a sign from me to take over your ship! It would have been done already if I hadn't noticed a nun's head dress.

BARRACHON: Sister Mary of the Angels!

(*He starts to stand up.*)

CHÉRI-BIBI: Ah! Don't jump around like that, my dear Captain. You might cause my revolver to go off just by itself. (*making him sit down again*) Here's my offer: I promise never again to bother my fellow citizens. We're not far from the coast of Africa. Put a slop at sea and let me go. That's all I'm asking! If that suits you, say so. You won't have Chéri-Bibi to fear any more. Not you, not anyone else. And with me gone, your ship will be safe. Why? Because without me, the other convicts are impotent. But if you refuse, beware! I'm not angry, but when attacked, I will defend myself.

(*Barrachon remains silent.*)

CHÉRI-BIBI: Well, do you have something to say? Is it yes? Is it no?

BARRACHON: (*firmly*) No!

CHÉRI-BIBI: Then so much the worse for you! Fatality!

BARRACHON: We'll see about that!

(*Barrachon rushes at Chéri-Bibi, who rapidly gains the upper hand and floors the Captain.*)

CHÉRI-BIBI: I'm not going to kill you, because I hate pointless crimes, but I swear to you that I will drop you off on the African coast, naked as a savage, to punish you for not having granted my last request! Good-bye for now, Captain!

(*Chéri-Bibi kicks the Captain away and escapes into the lower deck. After a couple of minutes, we hear rumbling coming from the interior of the ship, followed by several rifle shots.*)

BARRACHON: (*getting up*) Help! To arms!

(*More shots. Then, De Vilène returns, rushing onto the deck.*)

DE VILENE: The convicts are revolting!

BARRACHON: (*enraged*) Chéri-Bibi was here just now!

DE VILENE: (*shouting*) Alert!

(*Guards and sailors emerge from the lower decks and surround the Lieutenant and the Captain.*)

BARRACHON: How is Sister Mary?

DE VILENE: She came to. I discovered that she is Chéri-Bibi's sister.

BARRACHON: (*shocked*) His sister!

DE VILENE: She just confessed it to me. She thinks she's lost. Evidently, she spoke the truth.

(*Heavy firing begins. Pascaud enters, followed by some guards.*)

PASCAUD: Captain, we've lost control of the battery above, the one below and the third deck. Thirty of my men have already fallen. All the cages are open and nothing seems to stop these bandits.

BARRACHON: Sound the rally! All able-bodied men to the bridge!

PASCAUD: (*to a bugler*) Sound the muster!

(*The bugler pipes. In reply, we hear a loud shout: "Long live Chéri-Bibi!" A sailor enters, running from the lower decks; he has a large gash on his face.*)

SAILOR: They're attacking!

(*He collapses onto the deck. Suddenly, Sister Mary of the Angels enters. Her wound is such she can barely stand on her legs.*)

DE VILENE: Sister Mary?

BARRACHON: Please withdraw, Sister!

SISTER MARY: (*speaking with difficulty*) No, it's necessary that I be here. (calling Chéri-Bibi) Chéri-Bibi, listen to me! It's I, your sister. Have mercy on me. Chéri-Bibi, I still love you. In the name of Heaven, listen to me!

(*A new burst of firing.*)

DE VILENE: There's his reply.

SISTER MARY: If I die before you, know that I have forgiven you.

(*Renewed bursts of gunfire.*)

SISTER MARY: (*falling to her knees*) My God! Protect him! Protect him!

(*Night is now almost total.*)

BARRACHON: Watch out! They're coming!

SHOUTS: Long live Chéri-Bibi! Chéri-Bibi!

DE VILENE: Aim!

BARRACHON: Fire!

(*The fusillade begins; we hear screams, shouts, bugle calls. Many sailors roll on the deck.*)

PASCAUD: Captain! We can't hold them back!

BARRACHON: Fall back on the steerage and we'll try to catch them between two fires.

(*At the very moment, La Ficelle emerges from the wheelhouse, leaps on the machine gun and trains it on the bridge.*)

LA FICELLE: Too late!

DE VILENE: (*enraged*) Traitor!

(*Suddenly, the convicts emerge; at their head is the Countess, disheveled, armed with an axe; she is followed by Petit-Bon-Dieu, Le Kanak, Gueule-de-Bois, Le Rouquin, and others, swearing oaths, shouting, etc. The battle rages on for a while, then...*)

PETIT-BON-DIEU: The ship's on fire!

(*Flames are seen in the distance; Chéri-Bibi appears next to La Ficelle.*)

ALL THE CONVICTS: (*shouting*) Long live Chéri-Bibi!

(The Captain, the Lieutenant and the surviving sailors are now at the mercy of the convicts. Sister Mary of the Angels is in a corner, praying.)

CHÉRI-BIBI: Stop! We've won!

ALL THE CONVICTS: Long Live Chéri-Bibi!

CHÉRI-BIBI: Raise our flag.

(*The black flag goes up the mast.*)

CHÉRI-BIBI: (*victorious*) This is the black flag of pi-rates–the flag of Chéri-Bibi!

CURTAIN

SCENE III
MASTERS OF THE *BAYARD*

The rear bridge of the Bayard. The set is designed as a cut-away including a large cabin (the Captain's quarters) and the rest of the bridge. To both the left and the right, the bridge is limited by netting. Further back, there is a large cabin whose portholes have been opened to provide more air; it is furnished in an English style. On each side are two uncovered corridors. Further back, in silhouette, we see the great sail, smokestacks and the ocean. On the stage, there is an armchair and several wicker tables. It is 2 p.m. under a tropical Sun.

AT RISE, Chéri-Bibi is in the cabin, dressed in a Captain's uniform, writing, his back turned to the audience. La Ficelle, dressed as an Ensign, enters from one of the corridors leading to the bridge.

LA FICELLE: Captain, the second mate's just relieved the navigator.

CHÉRI-BIBI: (*without turning*) Ah?

LA FICELLE: From what it appears, we've gone down a few degrees too many to the South.

CHÉRI-BIBI: (*still not turning*) Ah?

LA FICELLE: Captain, how nice you look in that uniform!

CHÉRI-BIBI: You like it? You, too, look very nice

LA FICELLE: Yes, but I'm not as handsome as you. I never thought Captain Barrachon's uniform would look so good on you!

CHÉRI-BIBI: Ah, but am I not Captain Barrachon?

LA FICELLE: Yes, of course! What have you done with Chéri-Bibi, Captain?

CHÉRI-BIBI: He's in his cell and he will stay there! (*a pause*) We owe you our freedom, my brave La Ficelle! You're the one who gave us weapons and hid the Countess and I after our escape.

LA FICELLE: I didn't embark on the *Bayard* as a scullion to twirl my thumbs!

CHÉRI-BIBI: Thus, one more time, you wanted to link your fate to mine. You, an honest lad, wanted to share the misfortune of a convict like Chéri-Bibi.

LA FICELLE: Because I know you're innocent.

CHÉRI-BIBI: Innocent! (*despairing*) Am I? I've begun to doubt it myself. To such a degree that, for eight years I've shouted it in vain to the face of the world. But by living with bandits, have I not become like them? Perhaps worse than them? I've become a brute, following only the vilest instincts of violence, theft, murder!

LA FICELLE: (*in a tone of gentle reproach*) Then you no longer think of Mademoiselle Bourrelier–Cécily?

CHÉRI-BIBI: (*whose eyes fill with tears*) Cécily, Cécily!

LA FICELLE: You still love her?

CHÉRI-BIBI: Always! For life! (*baring his breast*) Heavens! I had her name engraved on my flesh, just as she's engraved in my heart.

LA FICELLE: (*reading the tattoo*) "To Cécily for life, Chéri-Bibi."

CHERI BIBI: And I love her with a mad love which is without hope, since I must never see her again. Besides, were I to see her again, my innocence recognized, rehabilitated at last, I could only flee her, because she is not free!

LA FICELLE: That's right! She married Maxime du Touchais.

CHÉRI-BIBI: Yes, this Maxime whom she appeared to detest and yet, upon whom she threw herself the second day after her father's death.

LA FICELLE: Doesn't that haste seem strange to you?

CHÉRI-BIBI: When one has seen what I've seen, when one has suffered what I've suffered, nothing seems strange anymore!

(*Gueule-de-Bois puts his head through the door at the back. He, too, is dressed like an officer.*)

GUEULE-DE-BOIS: Can I come in? I want to make a report. The discipline on board in general is terrible, but in particular with respect to Petit-Bon-Dieu. He objects every time I give him an order and spends his time indulging himself like a pig!

CHÉRI-BIBI: Make yourself obeyed at any price! I want the rules to be rigorously observed, understood? (*a pause*) A cigarette, Lieutenant?

GUEULE-DE-BOIS: A smoke? That's not to be refused, Captain.

(*Petit-Bon-Dieu, dressed as a Quarter-Master, enters from one of the corridors of the bridge.*)

PETIT-BON-DIEU: (*timidly*) Captain, I need to ask you something on behalf of the Countess.

CHÉRI-BIBI: What does she want?

PETIT-BON-DIEU: A moment of your time.

CHÉRI-BIBI: All my moments belong to the whole community. I haven't the right to indulge in any distractions, especially listening to some gossip.

GUEULE-DE-BOIS: But, Captain, remember that, after La Ficelle, the Countess was really useful to us.

CHÉRI-BIBI: You all get caught by her beauty like moths to the flame!

GUEULE-DE-BOIS: Perhaps, but she's caught you too!

CHÉRI-BIBI: (*threateningly*) Mind your words, Gueule-de-Bois. Le Kanak is my friend, and the wife of a friend is sacred!

PETIT-BON-DIEU: He's always had good morals, our Captain.

CHÉRI-BIBI: The women aboard my ship will be treated with respect. If you're not dead at this time, you owe it to Sister Mary.

GUEULE-DE-BOIS: I'll never forget it. And to prove it, last night, I watched over her again in the company of our ship doctor, Le Kanak!

CHÉRI-BIBI: How is she, this morning?

GUEULE-DE-BOIS: Much better. As her lungs were not harmed, there's nothing to fear. She can now get up.

CHÉRI-BIBI: Ah! (*he remains pensive for a moment*) So, nothing new. The gentlemen of the guard are enjoying their new position?

PETIT-BON-DIEU: They don't dare complain, Captain! Anyone who does, I will boil in oil

CHÉRI-BIBI: (*abruptly*) Leave me now.

(*They leave by the door at the back after giving a military salute. Then, Sister Mary enters by one of the corridors. She can be seen to shiver. Very moved, Chéri-Bibi rushes toward her, grasps her hands and throws himself at her feet.*)

CHÉRI-BIBI: (*choked up*) My little Jacqueline! My little Jacqueline!

SISTER MARY: Chéri-Bibi!

(*She gently raises him.*)

CHÉRI-BIBI: If you've come, it's because you've forgiven me.

SISTER MARY: I'd already forgiven you. Since your conviction, I haven't stopped praying for you. When you were caught after your first escape, I volunteered to go serve in the hospital in Cayenne to be near you.

CHÉRI-BIBI: (*very moved*) My little sister Jacqueline.

SISTER MARY: I am Sister Mary of the Angels now.

CHÉRI-BIBI: To me, you will always be my little Jacqueline who played with me in the perfumed garden by the sea, in those happy days of Spring in Normandy.

SISTER MARY: Yes... Do you remember when we came back from school and used to say good evening to all the good women mending the nets on their door steps?

CHÉRI-BIBI: And the coastline with its flowers and its butterflies...

SISTER MARY: ...The cliffs, the white sails, the gulls, the wind, the old clock at the chapel which rang when a sailor was lost at sea... Oh, Jean... Chéri-Bibi... (*she bursts into tears*) I've asked God's pardon, but despite everything, I haven't forgotten those days, the blessed hours of our childhood. Because I can't forget you committed your first crime because of me...

CHÉRI-BIBI: (*wildly*) You, too! You still think that I lied! Yet, you know me better than anyone else. You saw me every day, you read my eyes like a book. And yet, you're like the rest of them! You believe me guilty of the of Monsieur Bourrelier! I've written to you fifty times about what happened. I swore to you that I'm innocent!

SISTER MARY: I believe you, but as I said, even if you had killed him, I couldn't be angry with you! Before God, I took all responsibility for that crime.

CHÉRI-BIBI: If I'd done it, I wouldn't bother hiding it. On the contrary, I would boast of it! That's what you don't understand, Jacqueline! What the judges didn't understand either. It's for this very reason that I'm always looking for the man with the grey hat, who is the true murderer and for whose crime I have been unjustly condemned!

SISTER MARY: I knew it wasn't you who killed the Marquis du Touchais either. There's some new evidence...

CHÉRI-BIBI: Fatality wished that that I become a murderer in the eyes of the woman I love! It's frightful! But tell me about that new evidence. Is anyone seeking to acquit me of this second crime?

SISTER MARY: Yes. Someone you knew very well. Reine, the Marquise's aged governess.

CHÉRI-BIBI: Reine knows the real culprit?

SISTER MARY: Yes. One night, bad weather surprised me during one of my errands, and I was forced to spend the night at the Marquise's villa. There, old Reine came into my room, gripped by a strange exaltation, and said to me: "Poor Jacqueline! Your brother is innocent! It wasn't he who killed the Marquis, it was someone else."

CHÉRI-BIBI: She said that!

SISTER MARY: Yes, she even added that she would speak of it when the hour comes, but that if you knew the reasons that prevented her from speaking now, you would be the first to order her to remain silent...

CHÉRI-BIBI: She might die...

SISTER MARY: She's arranged everything, so that the truth will become known when the hour comes.

CHÉRI-BIBI: When the hour comes... (*shrugging*) Perhaps it will come too late!

(*La Ficelle enters from the bridge.*)

LA FICELLE: Captain! The lookout has spotted a wreck several miles off starboard. Distress signals are coming from it. What should we do?

CHÉRI-BIBI: Head towards it and increase speed!

LA FICELLE: Aye, Captain!

(*He leaves.*)

CHÉRI-BIBI: (*after a pause*) What about Cécily? Is she happy (*with effort*) since her marriage?

SISTER MARY: Alas, no! Before his marriage, Maxime du Touchais wasn't worth much, and the years haven't improved him.

CHÉRI-BIBI: But with Monsieur Bourrelier's millions, surely he leads a happy life?

SISTER MARY: It isn't that. He forced his mother and his wife to leave the Chateau du Touchais in order to publicly install his mistress there.

CHÉRI-BIBI: That's abominable!

SISTER MARY: So Cécily returned to the villa Bourrelier, with the Dowager Marquise.

CHÉRI-BIBI: What a scandal!

SISTER MARY: And what an affront for poor Cécily! That villainous woman took over the Marquise's estate, with her carriages, her motorcars. The Parisians who go to spend their summer vacations in Dieppe every year call her the "Star of Dieppe." And now, that's also the name of the Marquis du Touchais' new yacht.

CHÉRI-BIBI: What type of woman is she?

SISTER MARY: What they call a "woman of the world" or a "demi-mondaine." Her name is Sonia. She's from Poland originally. She now lives at the chateau—with her husband.

CHÉRI-BIBI: With her husband! What ignominy! What about poor Cécily then?

SISTER MARY: She's consoling herself by raising her son, Petit Bernard.

CHERI BIBI: How old is he?

SISTER MARY: Six, I believe. Happily, Cécily has not completely abandoned! The Marquise is very good to her, and also Monsieur de Pont-Marie, a friend of Maxime who often goes to visit her.

CHÉRI-BIBI: (*remembering*) Vicomte de Pont-Marie... A friend of Maxime...

SISTER MARY: He has changed much and made amends for the mistakes of his youth. He has even kept away from the Marquis, who, when I left, was preparing to go on a cruise with his friends in his yacht.

(*Gueule-de-Bois enters.*)

GUEULE-DE-BOIS: Captain! The wreck is now in sight! (*offering a pair of binoculars*) Look!

CHÉRI-BIBI: (*taking the binoculars, and grumbling*) A shipwreck! As if the cages weren't crowded enough! (*he looks through the binoculars muttering incomprehensible words, then, with a strange exaltation, murmurs*) Fatality!

(*Meanwhile, the convicts, dressed up as sailors, come onto the bridge. Sister Mary leaves by the back.*)

GUEULE-DE-BOIS: What do we do, Captain?

CHÉRI-BIBI: We're going to rescue them. Everyone must remember his new station! Don't make any mistakes! Nothing important happened on board since the *Bayard* left the Isle of Re, except for one revolt by the convicts, who was quickly suppressed! I'm Captain Barrachon, and the real Barrachon has become Chéri-Bibi. (*to Gueule-de-Bois*) Lieutenant de Vilène, you will greet the castaways on my behalf as they board. I will then come out to greet them in person. (*aside*) Is fate turning my way?

(*He leaves.*)

GUEULE-DE-BOIS: You heard the Captain! No fooling around! The first one out of step hangs high and fast!

LE ROUQUIN: (*leaning over the netting, looking at the castaways*) Hey! There's some gals over there!

PETIT-BON-DIEU: Goddesses, you mean!

LA FICELLE (*shouting to the helmsman*) Bear Starboard all the way!

LE ROUQUIN: They look like whores!

LA FICELLE: (*shouting*) Gently! Slacken up a quarter!

PETIT-BON-DIEU: There she is; the sloop is coming along side.

GUEULE-DE-BOIS: Lower down the ladder.

(*The convicts, dressed as sailors, execute the different maneuvers.*)

LA ROUQUIN: Ain't that nice! It's all going swell!

LA FICELLE: You can thank Chéri-Bibi!

GUEULE-DE-BOIS: Attention! They're coming up!

(*Baron Proskoff, around 40, rakish looking, appears.*)

GUEULE-DE-BOIS: Welcome aboard the *Bayard*, Sir.

PROSKOFF: (*introducing himself*) I'm Baron Proskoff. Words fail me to thank you, our saviors.

(*A very pretty blonde woman is hoisted aboard.*)

PROSKOFF: (*introducing her*) And this is Mademoiselle Nadja de Valrieu, a very famous dramatic actress.

GUEULE-DE-BOIS: (*aside*) Holy Cow! I'd really like to get to know her better.

PETIT-BON-DIEU: (*aside, to Le Rouquin*) Just see how excited Gueule-de-Bois is!

LE ROUQUIN: It's not just him!

(*Now, an equally beautiful brunette is hoisted aboard.*)

PROSKOFF: And this is Mademoiselle Carmen de Fontainebleau, the celebrated artistic dancer.

(*Congratulations, handshaking all around.*)

PETIT-BON-DIEU: (*to Gueule-de-Bois, pointing to Carmen*) You see that gal, there? She's just my type! If she would–if it weren't too expensive...

GUEULE-DE-BOIS: (*pointing to a man coming aboard with great difficulty*) Eh! Your last companion seems to be ill.

PROSKOFF: This is our friend, the Marquis Maxime du Touchais, who owned the yacht we were on when the storm struck. He is indeed ill.

(*Maxime climbs aboard.*)

MAXIME: Please excuse me for not being the first to introduce myself, as would have been my duty, but I'm ill...

GUEULE-DE-BOIS: We'll get you back to your feet in no time. (*To Le Kanak, dressed as Ship Surgeon*) Major, will you please see to Monsieur le Marquis? (*to the sailors*) Help the Major take our guest to the infirmary!

MAXIME: Thank you, gentlemen, for your solicitude on my behalf.

(*Maxime, supported by two sailors, leaves, followed by Le Kanak.*)

GUEULE-DE-BOIS: And now, my dear Baron, would you tell us the details of your shipwreck? (*to Carmen and Nadja*) Ladies, please, I beg you to sit down

PROSKOFF: My story, gentlemen, will be very brief. We were returning to France on the *Star of Dieppe*–that's the name of the Marquis' yacht–when, two night ago, because of a storm, we collided with a larger boat, which caused considerable damage to ours. The *Star of Dieppe* started to take water. Our situation became critical. The life boats were put in the sea. We took refuge in them, but death seemed as certain on these frail craft as on the yacht itself...

CARMEN: So much so that, all things being equal, Maxime chose to stay on his ship.

PROSKOFF: My two companions and I went back on the yacht to convince him to come with us, but in vain. We had just accepted this decision when, suddenly, the yacht stopped sinking.

GUEULE-DE-BOIS: I guess the watertight bulkhead must have held firm.

PROSKOFF: Indeed. So much so that we were able to wait for a while before risking our lives again in a life boat.

NADJA: Get to the point. You're not telling *The Odyssey*.

PROSKOFF: Right! Well, luck then put you on our path. Luckily for Maxime who, from emotion or a cold, had developed a nasty fever.

GUEULE-DE-BOIS: So all's well that ends well.

PROSKOFF: My joy at being rescued is only marred by the fact that my wife, my dearest Sonia, stubbornly insisted on getting into one of those fragile lifeboats and, at this moment, I am, perhaps, a widower.

(*The convicts come to shake his hand.*)

NADJA: My poor darling, you must let go...

CARMEN: Yes. Don't afflict yourself. We'll find ways of consoling you.

(*Chéri-Bibi, dressed in his Captain uniform, enters from the rear.*)

CHERI-BIBI: Ladies, Sir... I'm Captain Barrachon and I'm pleased to welcome you aboard the *Bayard*.

(*The Baron, Nadja and Carmen rush to shake his hand.*)

PROSKOFF: Captain, we owe you our lives!

CHÉRI-BIBI: Don't mention it. I just came from the infirmary where our doctor is caring for the Marquis du Touchais. He hopes it will be nothing.

PROSKOFF: So much the better. If you knew what a *bon-vivant* our Marquis is...

CARMEN:(*pointing to two convicts, one has a bandage on his head, the other his arm in a sling*) It looks like you've been into battle, Captain!

CHÉRI-BIBI: You couldn't put it better, Mademoiselle. Indeed, we have been into battle; we had a revolt on board!

NADJA: A revolt on board! Oh! Do tell us about it!

PROSKOFF: A revolt aboard a military ship? Is it possible? Is there no discipline in our navy? I hope, Captain, that you didn't have too much trouble overcoming the mutineers?

CHÉRI-BIBI: Well, it was necessary to shoot a few.

CARMEN: Why, that's very interesting. A shipwreck! A mutiny! Such adventures!

NADJA: We sure won't lack for topics of conversation when we return to France.

CHÉRI-BIBI: I'm afraid it won't be too soon, tomorrow, Mesdemoiselles, because Cayenne is our destination.

PROSKOFF: Cayenne! Devil's Island! You give me the shivers, Captain!

CHÉRI-BIBI: I apologize, Baron. We are carrying a full shipload of convicts, kept in metal cages. It's those dogs who gave us a good deal of trouble earlier.

CARMEN: Convicts! Criminals!

NADJA: Ah! My God! At least, they cannot do us any harm.

CHÉRI-BIBI: Have no fear, Mademoiselle, we've got them locked up now. They won't get out of their cages. And the first one who makes a move will get his head blown off. (*noticing the girls' scared expressions*) Oh! Pardon! Excuse me!

PROSKOFF: Don't apologize, Captain! We're much too good towards those beasts! If we had a real government, I bet most of them would have already been guillotined.

CHÉRI-BIBI: At least half, you are right, Baron. And of course, we're also transporting a notorious criminal–the infamous Chéri-Bibi.

PROSKOFF: What? Cheri-Bibi is on board?

NADJA: Is it true, Captain? You have Chéri-Bibi prisoner on this ship?

CARMEN: Ah! What luck! Show him to us, please Captain!

CHÉRI-BIBI: (*laughing*) For dessert, perhaps. Lunch is being served and you must be hungry.

NADJA: But afterward, we will see Chéri-Bibi?

CHÉRI-BIBI: As you see me, beautiful lady.

(*The fake sailors have set a finely dressed table. The Countess enters, dressed elegantly.*)

CHÉRI-BIBI: Ladies, my dear Baron, allow me to present to you the Comtesse (*hesitating*) de Canaque.

(*Greetings, congratulations.*)

COUNTESS: My dear Captain, I learned of the happy event that brings these ladies aboard, and I am coming to put my cabin at their disposal. It's the best on the *Bayard*.

NADJA: We wouldn't dream of disturbing you...

CARMEN: It's very kind but we can't allow...

CHÉRI-BIBI: (*cutting matters short*) To the table!

(*He places himself in the middle, between Nadja and Carmen. On one side, the Baron and the Countess. La Ficelle, Gueule-de-Bois take their places. Le Rouquin, Petit-Bon-Dieu and the other convicts remain seated.*)

NADJA: (*to the Countess*) Would it be indiscreet to ask you, Countess, why you took passage on this ship?

COUNTESS: Not at all. In my leisure, I am a woman of letters, and as such, I feel I cannot be ignorant of any environment.

CHÉRI-BIBI: I must tell you that this little banquet which I am giving in your honor, is not very proper, but, aboard the *Bayard*, we are like a family.

PROSKOFF: It's extraordinary, that air of resemblance between you all.

NADJA: Doubtless, that comes from all of you being shaved.

CARMEN: (*bursting into laughter*) Just like convicts!

(*There is a very pregnant pause.*)

LE ROUQUIN: How amusing!

PETIT-BON-DIEU: Yes, she's very funny. (*slapping his thigh.*)

(*Burst of genial laughter from the convicts.*)

CHÉRI-BIBI: It is precisely to set a good example to the convicts that we all shave our heads.

PETIT-BON-DIEU: Yes, our Captain doesn't need a load of bollocks...

PROSKOFF: "Bollocks"?

LA FICELLE: Er, it's navy slang for the rules.

CHÉRI-BIBI: And, ladies, don't think that because I allow my men to treat me like their father, that disciplines suffers for it. I know how to be severe when necessary. If I didn't use force as well as heart, after the revolt of the other day, we would be the ones in the cages right now.

LE ROUQUIN: Bravo!

GUEULE-DE-BOIS: Shut up, Le Rouquin! (*to the Baron*) We've known each other for so long, that we call each other by our nicknames!

PROSKOFF: (*aside, to Carmen*) What colorful characters!

CARMEN: (*dryly*) They're a riot.

(*Le Kanak enters.*)

CHÉRI-BIBI: Ah! How's our patient, Doctor?

LE KANAK: Better. A simple chill. He'll have to stay in bed for a few days.

PROSKOFF: Poor Maxime. Truly, he has no luck. He loses his yacht, he's sick, and all the while, his wife is making a cuckold of him.

CHÉRI-BIBI: (*automatically*) That can't be true!

(*General stupefaction.*)

COUNTESS: (*in control*) What is it you said, Captain?

CHÉRI-BIBI: (*non-plussed*) What? I didn't say anything.

COUNTESS: (*to Baron*) I must tell you that our Captain is like a true knight!. No one can criticize women in front of him!

CARMEN: In any case, if Maxime isn't yet what he fears to be, it won't be long before he is.

NADJA: The Marquise has no taste! The last time that I saw her in Dieppe, she was returning from the races. She was wearing such a terrible hat!

CARMEN: She dresses like a provincial.

CHÉRI-BIBI: (*hardly able to contain himself, rises abruptly*) I regret to interrupt this little chat so suddenly, but I have orders to give. (*to Carmen and Nadja*) Besides, you must be in need of rest?

CARMEN: Certainly. But you promised to show us Chéri-Bibi?

NADJA: Before this evening?

CHÉRI-BIBI: (*ominously*) Indeed, I promise you!

(*All rise and leave by the corridors of the bridge, as the convicts rapidly clear the table.*)

CHÉRI-BIBI: (*to the Countess just as she's about to leave*) Stay! I need to speak to you.

COUNTESS: (*once they are alone*) What's wrong? What's got into you?

CHÉRI-BIBI: Listen. (*suddenly grasping both her hands*) Listen carefully. I know that you love me, Countess.

COUNTESS: That's true. But I know it's not reciprocated.

CHÉRI-BIBI: Since you love me, are you prepared to do something for me?

COUNTESS: Anything you want!

CHÉRI-BIBI: Then tell me what you did with the strips of human flesh that you and Le Kanak tore away from your victims. Tell me!

COUNTESS: (*with a gesture of horror*) That–never!

CHÉRI-BIBI: So there are things you won't do for me.

COUNTESS: Why do you want to know?

CHÉRI-BIBI: Because I'm thinking of giving you some one to torture, to make him suffer...

COUNTESS: What did he do to you, the one upon whom you want to avenge yourself?

CHÉRI-BIBI: He tore out my heart. And beyond that, he's got everything. He's rich, very rich...

COUNTESS: He's that rich?

CHÉRI-BIBI: He's worth millions! What do you think? Why are you turning your head away? Why are your cheeks so pale, your eyes so somber? What's wrong with you?

COUNTESS: Nothing, nothing.

CHÉRI-BIBI: I want to know what you're thinking!

COUNTESS: It's our secret, Le Kanak's and mine. A secret which, if divulged, could lead us to the guillotine! So, now you understand why I can't tell you anything about it.

CHÉRI-BIBI: You're playing with me ! You don't love me!

COUNTESS: It's precisely because I do love you that you won't learn anything from me. If Le Kanak wants to confide his secret to you, that's his business! But, consider carefully, Chéri-Bibi. If you ever speak of it, you will cause two heads to fall. Mine belongs you, if you want to take it.

(*She leans toward him amorously.*)

CHÉRI-BIBI: (*after a pause*) Lead me to Le Kanak. I will speak to him.

(*They leave by the door at the back. The stage remains empty for a moment, then Baron Proskoff, Nadja, and Carmen enter from one of the corridors with an air of mystery about them, and make sure they are alone.*)

PROSKOFF: Since we set foot on this ship, we've gone from one mystery to another.

CARMEN: This crew certainly behaves strangely.

NADJA: It's worrying. I can't help having the shivers.

CARMEN: A shiver is something delightful. I wouldn't mind a bit of a scare myself.

NADJA: I'd like to know what's going on. I'd feel safer. What about you, Baron?

PROSKOFF: Indeed. But I can't tell you anything because I don't know anything. (*controlling himself*) But I won't be afraid.

(*Gueule-de-Bois enters, followed by Petit-Bon-Dieu, Le Rouquin, La Ficelle and a few other convicts, still dressed as sailors.*)

GUEULE-DE-BOIS: Are our guests pleased? Have all your wishes been fulfilled?

(*Nadja, Carmen, and the Baron huddle against each other.*)

NADJA: (*jabbing Carmen with an elbow*) Answer him!

CARMEN: (*elbowing Nadja*) You answer him!

PROSKOFF: (*stammering*) You–you were saying, Lieutenant?

GUEULE-DE-BOIS: I asked if all your wishes have been satisfied?

PROSKOFF: Why, certainly. Isn't that so, ladies?

NADJA: Right, Carmen?

(*Carmen makes an evasive gesture.*)

GUEULE-DE-BOIS: Yet, I see that the ladies appear a bit embarrassed. That means we haven't granted all their wishes. But we're going to remedy this at once. (*to a convict*) Go get Chéri-Bibi.

PROSKOFF: No need to. Don't bother. The ladies don't think it's that important any more, right, ladies?

CARMEN: Right, Nadja?

(*Carmen and Nadja seem very embarrassed.*)

GUEULE-DE-BOIS: No, no, no. A promise is a promise. Go get Chéri-Bibi, you two.

(*Two convicts leave.*)

GUEULE-DE-BOIS: You're going to see this terrible bandit whose crimes captivated public opinion.

PROSKOFF: (*blandly*) What a treat (*aside to Carmen and Nadja*) One that I'd rather forego. What a crazy idea you had back there.

(*Captain Barrachon enters, dressed as a convict. His bonnet bears the number 3216.*)

GUEULE-DE-BOIS: Ladies, allow me to present to you the infamous Chéri-Bibi!

NADJA: Well! Truly. This is not the way I pictured him at all.

CARMEN: Me, neither.

PROSKOFF: He looks more like a badly dressed notary.

BARRACHON: (*abruptly*) I'm Captain Barrachon. I was locked in a cage like the rest of my crew when the convicts seized the ship. (*pointing to Gueule-de-Bois*) As for him, he's no more Lieutenant de Vilène than I am Chéri-Bibi. He's the convict Gueule-de-Bois...

(*The Baron, Carmen and Nadja huddle against each other, trembling. Chéri-Bibi returns suddenly.*)

CHÉRI-BIBI: That's right!

PROSKOFF: Ah, Dear God!

(*He falls into the arms of Carmen and Nadja, who screams.*)

CHÉRI-BIBI: Silence, my little bird! I repeat my order that no harm is to be done to the crew of the *Bayard*–nor to the castaways that fate has sent to us.

(*Murmurs of disapproval amongst the convicts.*)

CHÉRI-BIBI: Silence! I've made up my mind to disembark them safe and sound at a place to be determined.

(*Protests.*)

CHÉRI-BIBI: Who dares raise his voice when I'm talking?

(*Immediate silence.*)

CHÉRI-BIBI: The Marquis du Touchais, whom we brought aboard, has purchased the freedom of his friends for the sum of 5 million francs.

(*Stupor, then delirious enthusiasm.*)

CHÉRI-BIBI: Friends! The deal I made is quite clear: we'll release the Marquis and his friends unharmed only if we're paid the five millions. It's either five millions—or death. Now, leave me alone with my staff.

(*The convicts drag off Captain Barrachon, the Baron, Carmen and Nadja. Gueule-de-Bois, Petit-Bon-Dieu, Le Rouquin and La Ficelle remain behind.*)

CHÉRI-BIBI: La Ficelle, approach. Land will soon be in sight. At night fall, you will disembark.

LA FICELLE: Me?

CHÉRI-BIBI: I'm putting you in charge of getting the five millions. (*he hands him a portfolio*) You will find here the list of banks and the signatures required for you to obtain the money.

A VOICE: Land on the Starboard!

CHÉRI-BIBI: You have five minutes to prepare for your departure.

LA FICELLE: Good-bye, everybody!

GUEULE-DE-BOIS: You've been invested with a position of trust.

LE ROUQUIN: Complete your mission and get back to us in a hurry.

PETIT-BON-DIEU: And you'd better not run off with the loot!

LA FICELLE: Good-bye, Chéri-Bibi.

CHÉRI-BIBI: (*deeply moved*) Goodbye, La Ficelle. (*low and quickly*) You will go and see Cécily. Look at her carefully. Kiss her for me with your eyes, and when you return, tell me if she is still as beautiful as ever. Go, hug me, my friend. (*they embrace.*)

CURTAIN

SCENE IV
NOT HIS HANDS!

A deserted island in Malaysia. A clearing in a virgin forest near the sea. Facing the audience, there is a low hut, roughly constructed, the entire interior of which can be seen. It has two doors. One communicates with the exterior. A second with another hut. The back is closed by a rough curtain. This hut, having no windows, is always plunged in darkness. Outside, there are several casks and barrels, then the jungle. It is dawn.

AT RISE, the hut is empty. Le Rouquin stands guard before the door. Gueule-de-Bois enters from the first hut, followed by Petit-Bon-Dieu.

GUEULE-DE-BOIS: Everything OK, Le Rouquin?

LE ROUQUIN: Yes, Lieutenant. The night went off without incidents.

GUEULE-DE-BOIS: Nothing suspicious in the attitude of Le Kanak or the Countess?

LE ROUQUIN: Neither has emerged all night.

PETIT-BON-DIEU: No screams? No complaints?

LE ROUQUIN: Several times, I thought I recognized the voice of Chéri-Bibi, then the Marquis. I was unable to understand their words, but it

sounded like a groaning. It seemed to me he
was complaining about his hands.

GUEULE-DE-BOIS: You didn't observe anything else?

LE ROUQUIN: No, nothing.

GUEULE-DE-BOIS: Keep up the watch. I'll have you
relieved in an hour.

LE ROUQUIN: I won't say no to that, because I'm beginning to feel rusty here, and I would really
like to explore this beautiful island, like the
rest of our comrades.

PETIT-BON-DIEU: Gueule-de-Bois put you in charge
because he trusts you.

LE ROUQUIN: I'm honored–but a little angry too. I
don't want to face Le Kanak. He's no longer
my friend. You won't get the idea out of my
head that he had something to do with Chéri-
Bibi's illness.

GUEULE-DE-BOIS: Be patient, Le Rouquin. Think that
soon, you will share in the five millions ransom!

PETIT-BON-DIEU: We'll live like kings!

LE ROUQUIN: I'm really counting on it–but I'd also
like to know what's going on!

PETIT-BON-DIEU: (*to Gueule-de-Bois*) The fellow's got a point. What are we to make of what's going on?

GUEULE-DE-BOIS: I don't know anything more than you do! I'm tired of all this secrecy too! Since La Ficelle left, the condition of the Marquis du Touchais has worsened, despite the efforts of Le Kanak and the Countess...

PETIT-BON-DIEU: And then, Le Kanak tells us that Chéri-Bibi has caught the same fever from the Marquis...

LE ROUQUIN: I tell you, it's not natural.

GUEULE-DE-BOIS: And we've been forbidden to see him, since he's been quarantined. Even more reason to talk to him...

PETIT-BON-DIEU: Then, Le Kanak pretends that his patients can't endure the sea...

LE ROUQUIN: ...And we disembark here, on this deserted island in Malaysia.

GUEULE-DE-BOIS: And in the five months since we've been here, no one has been able to see Chéri-Bibi. I'm just as concerned as you are —and quite tired of it too!

PETIT-BON-DIEU: I agree. We need to have an explanation with Le Kanak. But you know how he is; if he doesn't want to talk, he'll never talk.

GUEULE-DE-BOIS: So much the worse for him then. In the absence of Chéri-Bibi, I'm in charge, and I know how to make my authority respected–even by Le Kanak.

LE ROUQUIN: Well said, Gueule-de-Bois!

(*At the moment, Baron Proskoff, Nadja and Carmen enter from the jungle.*)

PETIT-BON-DIEU: We should have locked them up in a cage

GUEULE-DE-BOIS: Chéri-Bibi gave his word. Since the Marquis agreed to pay their ransom, they're not prisoners, but hostages.

PROSKOFF: (*coming forward*) Excuse me, my good man...

GUEULE-DE-BOIS: Couldn't you call me Lieutenant? Does it burn your mouth to give me my title?

PROSKOFF: My apologies, Lieutenant. The Ladies and I were desirous of knowing if we are to remain prisoners much longer.

GUEULE-DE-BOIS: I know nothing about it. So you don't like our island? Look at the trees and the flowers. I think it's not lacking in natural beauty.

CARMEN: Well, it's not as nice as the Avenue du Bois de Boulogne.

PROSKOFF: For an island, it's not bad; but the only distraction we have is to tour it. It's easily done in one day, and it's been exactly 30 days since we've come ashore. So we've toured it 30 times. You will admit that's a bit tiresome.

NADJA: If only it had a casino.

GUEULE-DE-BOIS: Rejoice! Your captivity is about to end. Recently, I sent the steam sloop to the rendezvous point agreed upon to meet La Ficelle, whom we are expecting to return any day now. If, indeed, the Marquis has not deceived us, you can look forward to your repatriation very soon.

PROSKOFF: So you are going to get the five millions. What a godsend.

PETIT-BON-DIEU: It'll make things much easier, that's for sure.

PROSKOFF: If you don't mind a bit of advice, gentlemen, after you all become homeowners, beware of burglars. They're becoming very bold at the moment.

PETIT-BON-DIEU: Don't worry. We'll take our precautions.

PROSKOFF: Very good.

(*He prepares to leave with Nadja and Carmen.*)

LE ROUQUIN: Excellent advice.

GUEULE-DE-BOIS: (*calling them back*) Aren't you going to ask us for news of your friend the Marquis du Touchais?

PROSKOFF: Heavens! You're right!

CARMEN: That poor Maxime!

NADJA: We forgot about him.

PETIT-BON-DIEU: (*aside*) They only care as long as he foots the bill.

PROSKOFF: See you later, gentlemen.

(*Carmen, Nadja and the Baron leave.*)

LE ROUQUIN: (*to Petit-Bon-Dieu*) I saw you make tender eyes at the girls. You don't think you have a chance, do you?

PETIT-BON-DIEU: I'll tell you what. Now that they know we're going to be rich, I bet they're going to take a second look at us...

GUEULE-DE-BOIS: You really are disgusting. (*pause*) I'm going to speak to Le Kanak.

PETIT-BON-DIEU: I'll leave you to it. If it goes sour, call me and I'll be there to give you a hand. Besides, Le Rouquin will be here.

(*Petit-Bon-Dieu leaves.*)

GUEULE-DE-BOIS: (*to Le Rouquin*) Call Le Kanak and tell him that Gueule-de-Bois wants to speak with him.

LE ROUQUIN: Le Kanak! Le Kanak! (*silence from the hut*) He's not responding.

GUEULE-DE-BOIS: Then go in and bring him to me.

(*Just as Le Rouquin knocks on the door, Le Kanak emerges running form the door at the back. He's dressed in a hospital coat and is covered with blood.*)

LE KANAK: What is it?

LE ROUQUIN: Gueule-de-Bois wants to see you.

LE KANAK: I don't have time...

GUEULE-DE-BOIS: (*coming forward*) Open for me. You will see me all the same.

LE KANAK: (*excitedly*) Wait! (*calling low and rapidly*) Countess! Countess!

(*The Countess enters from the door at the back.*)

LE KANAK: Help me to take off my coat.

GUEULE-DE-BOIS: I'm waiting!

LE KANAK: (*aloud*) I'm coming. (*to the Countess, giving her his coat*) Take it and hide it.

(*The Countess takes the bloodied coat, rolls it up and leaves by the door at the back. Le Kanak appears in the doorway, dressed as a surgeon.*)

LE KANAK: I'm here.

GUEULE-DE-BOIS: You took your time. Pretty soon, it'll be necessary to request an audience with you, like a minister.

LE KANAK: What do you want, Gueule-de-Bois?

GUEULE-DE-BOIS: We're expecting La Ficelle back any time now.

LE KANAK: So?

GUEULE-DE-BOIS: So, decisions must be made.

LE KANAK: And?

GUEULE-DE-BOIS: And they can't be made without Chéri-Bibi. All the men are uneasy over his health. They can't remain any longer without knowing what's become of him. We want to see Chéri-Bibi.

LE KANAK: (*calm*) That's not possible.

GUEULE-DE-BOIS: I understand he can't see everyone, but let me see him, for five minutes and then everything will be all right.

LE KANAK: Not you, not anyone.

GUEULE-DE-BOIS: (*reasonable*) At least, let me speak to him through the door. He will talk to me.

LE KANAK: Right now, Chéri-Bibi can't talk.

GUEULE-DE-BOIS: Why's that?

LE KANAK: Because he's forbidden to speak.

GUEULE-DE-BOIS: Let him write to him then, so he can tell us what's happening, so he can reassure us! If it's something that shouldn't be told to the others, I can keep a secret.

LE KANAK: Chéri-Bibi can't write either.

GUEULE-DE-BOIS: Really? Are you making fun of me? Take care, Le Kanak; if you've harmed even a hair of our Chéri-Bibi, I'll kill you like a dog!

(*The Countess has listened to the exchange through the half open door. She now goes out and comes back on stage from the rear.*)

COUNTESS: (*appearing in the doorway*) Chéri-Bibi is asking to see Gueule-de-Bois.

GUEULE-DE-BOIS: Ah, you see!

COUNTESS: (*low to Le Kanak*) Have no fear, I've arranged everything.

LE KANAK: (*to Gueule-de-Bois*) What I did was motivated by his condition, which is serious, but if he's asking for you...

GUEULE-DE-BOIS: I'll come with you

(*The Countess and Le Kanak enter the hut, followed by Gueule-de-Bois.*)

GUEULE-DE-BOIS: Where is he?

(*The Countess pulls a cord: the curtains on the door in the back slide back and reveal two beds, side by side, their feet to the audience. Chéri-Bibi is in one, Maxime du Touchais in the other.*)

CHÉRI-BIBI: Is that you, Gueule-de-Bois?

GUEULE-DE-BOIS: My poor old friend! You've really been ill. But you're better now. Give me your hand.

LE KANAK: (*quickly*) No! No! You mustn't touch his hands!

CHÉRI-BIBI: It's forbidden.

GUEULE-DE-BOIS: I can barely see you in the dark. I Can't tell you apart from the Marquis.

COUNTESS: The Marquis is in a deep sleep.

GUEULE-DE-BOIS: I'd like to see how you look.

LE KANAK: No light! It's forbidden for the moment. Mustn't tire his eyes.

GUEULE-DE-BOIS: What was wrong with you, damn it?

CHÉRI-BIBI: I will tell you some other time. Let's speak of serious things, because Le Kanak doesn't want me to get tired.

GUEULE-DE-BOIS: It's hard to recognize your voice. You must have suffered so much.

CHÉRI-BIBI: You can tell all our comrades on my behalf that Le Kanak and the Countess have given me admirable care. I'll soon be up and about. Until then, you have my full powers.

LE KANAK: That's enough talk for now.

CHÉRI-BIBI: See you soon, Gueule-de-Bois.

GUEULE-DE-BOIS: See you soon, my poor friend.

(*Gueule-de-Bois heads toward the door with Le Kanak, while the Countess remains near Chéri-Bibi.*)

GUEULE-DE-BOIS: Between you and me, is it serious?

LE KANAK: Yes, very serious.

GUEULE-DE-BOIS: Can you save him?

LE KANAK: I hope so, but I doubt it.

GUEULE-DE-BOIS: What about the Marquis?

LE KANAK: The Marquis is less severely affected.

GUEULE-DE-BOIS: Our Chéri-Bibi could die! Oh! It must not be!

LE KANAK: Life is full of surprises.

GUEULE-DE-BOIS: Life? You're talking about death.

(*Gueule-de-Bois leaves. Le Kanak shuts the door after him and heads towards Chéri-Bibi.*)

LE KANAK: We've got to get this over with. How are you feeling?

CHÉRI-BIBI: Much better. But my hands still hurt. Why did you make me suffer so much?

LE KANAK: It was necessary.

CHÉRI-BIBI: No! Not the hands! It wasn't necessary.

COUNTESS: Chéri-Bibi, you know you mustn't speak.

CHÉRI-BIBI: (*pointing to the body beside him*) And him! He's been motionless for two days. What have you done to him?

LE KANAK: I'll explain later.

COUNTESS: Time presses.

LE KANAK: Come on! Get up (*emphasizing his words*) Monsieur le Marquis! And try to play your role well.

(*Meanwhile, outside, Baron Proskoff, Nadja and Carmen return from the forest.*)

PROSKOFF: Ladies, I tell you without false shame that I am exhausted..

NADJA: What an idea to climb up that tree like a monkey!

PROSKOFF: But it was to bring you some coconuts, my pretty.

CARMEN: Have you always been so gallant with women, Baron?

PROSKOFF: Always–except with mine, of course.

NADJA: Tell me, Baron, do you sometimes think about her?

PROSKOFF: About who?

CARMEN: About your wife!

PROSKOFF: Oh, her! Yes! I've never thought about her as much as now.

CARMEN: Is that because you hope to never to see her again?

PROSKOFF: I am certain that, if she escaped the ship-wreck, she is already consoling herself for my disappearance, which she assumes must be a *fait accompli*.

NADJA: And she's become a merry widow!

PROSKOFF: And as I no longer hope to be reunited with her...

CARMEN: ...You've become a merry widower too.

(*Several siren sounds. Le Rouquin, still on watch, looks toward the direction from which the sounds are coming.*)

ROUGIN: The steamer is coming.

PROSKOFF: Is that Monsieur La Ficelle?

CARMEN: Yes, I see him–at the rear.

NADJA: At last we're going to see Paris again!

PROSKOFF: I can't wait to see her again.

CARMEN: Who? Your wife?

PROSKOFF: No, silly! The Eiffel Tower! You cannot know the joy I feel when I look at the Eiffel Tower!

NADJA: Because you have artistic tastes.

PROSKOFF: (*with a sigh*) I'm looking forward to strolling down the *Grands Boulevards*, smoking my cigar between the Madeleine and the Faubourg Montmartre.

(*Shouts can be heard: "Long Live La Ficelle! Long Live La Ficelle!" La Ficelle enters and is quickly surrounded by Gueule-de-Bois, Petit-Bon-Dieu and the other convicts.*)

PROSKOFF: (*rushing forward*) You've succeeded!

LA FICELLE: Yes! (*to Gueule-de-Bois*) But first, I must see Chéri-Bibi.

GUEULE-DE-BOIS: That might be tricky. I told you he's been very sick. (*to Le Rouquin*) Call Le Kanak.

(*Le Rouquin raps on the door.*)

LA FICELLE: Never mind that. I must see him.

(*Le Kanak opens the door.*)

LE KANAK: What is it?

GUEULE-DE-BOIS: It's La Ficelle who's just returned, and insists on seeing Chéri-Bibi.

LE KANAK: It's impossible!

LA FICELLE: Look, Le Kanak, you can't stop me from seeing Chéri-Bibi.

LE KANAK: Unfortunately, I can.

LA FICELLE: (*uneasily*) Why?

LE KANAK: Because he's dead!

ALL: Dead!

(*La Ficelle pushes Le Kanak aside and enters the hut.*)

LA FICELLE: Chéri-Bibi can't be dead!

(*Le Kanak steps back and the others enter gradually.*)

LE KANAK: (*his back against the curtain*) He just died. Look, you can satisfy yourselves about it.

(*The curtains open and we see Chéri-Bibi dead in a bed, in the glow of a candle on a nightstand. On her knees by the bed, the Countess watches over him. Le Kanak makes everyone move out, then speaks to La Ficelle.*)

LE KANAK: Last night was bad; this morning, he was a bit better, when Gueule-de-Bois saw him. But soon after he left, the illness abruptly seized him again and he expired in our arms.

(*All kneel down.*)

LA FICELLE: My poor Chéri-Bibi! My poor Chéri-Bibi! To think that I came so far to learn such terrible news!

LE KANAK: (*pulling him away*) No point in staying here any longer.

LA FICELLE: Chéri-Bibi! Chéri-Bibi!

(*The curtains close. All leave the hut except for La Ficelle, Gueule-de-Bois, Petit-Bon-Dieu, Le Rouquin and the Countess.*)

GUEULE-DE-BOIS: We have decisions to make. Let's deliberate.

LE KANAK: Military honors should be rendered to our leader, and his glorious remains should buried at sea. As for the rest, here are Chéri-Bibi's last instructions. (*handing him a sealed envelope*) Read.

GUEULE-DE-BOIS: (*unsealing the letter and reading*) "In the event that La Ficelle's voyage is successful, here is what I have decided. The Marquis du Touchais will be deposited in a small port on the coast of Borneo; from there, he will return to France as he pleases. The other castaways, as well as former Captain Barrachon, the old crew and guards of the *Bayard*, will be disembarked on a desert island with two months supplies. You will notify the Australian authorities of their location so that they can come to rescue them. Signed: Chéri-Bibi." I will take steps to execute these orders. Le Rouquin and Petit-Bon-Dieu, come with me.

(*They leave.*)

LA FICELLE: What about the Marquis? You were able to save him but you weren't able to save our poor Chéri-Bibi?

COUNTESS: The Marquis is better, much better.

LA FICELLE: Fatality! That was Chéri-Bibi's motto.

LE KANAK: What about your mission?

LA FICELLE: Everything went well. The millions are in bank notes in my suitcase. Instead of five millions, I brought six. There's one for you, Le Kanak, according to the secret instructions I received from Chéri-Bibi. Keep it for yourself. No one will ever know about it! Take the rest and distribute it to the others. I don't want any of it myself.

(*We hear a distant salvo of gunfire.*)

LE KANAK: Gueule-de-Bois is rendering honors to our leader. Let's go back to the *Bayard*.

LA FICELLE: Leave me alone with my sorrow.

LE KANAK: As you will.

(*Le Kanak leaves with the Countess. La Ficelle remains for a moment with his head in his hands. From the door at the back, Chéri-Bibi, who, thanks to Le Kanak's surgical prowess, has now assumed the physical appearance of Maxime du Touchais enters slowly and touches the shoulder of La Ficelle who is in the slough of despair.*)

LA FICELLE: (*shivering*) Monsieur le Marquis.

CHÉRI-BIBI: La Ficelle, I know how cruel the loss you have just experienced is for you. Would you allow me to shake your hand?

LA FICELLE: (*stammering*) Yes, Monsieur.

(*They shake hands. Then Chéri-Bibi leaves by the door and reaches the forest.*)

LA FICELLE: (*ready to faint*) What's wrong with me? I can't look at the Marquis without becoming weak. Perhaps it's because his eyes strangely resemble those of Chéri-Bibi. It's as if I had felt he was still at my side. I hear a voice inside me screaming: "He isn't dead. Chéri-Bibi isn't dead."

(*He heads toward the rear and raises the curtain.*)

LA FICELLE: And yet his body is still here.

(*Noticing Le Kanak's blood-stained coat; he takes it and let the curtain fall back.*)

LA FICELLE: Blood–blood everywhere. What is it that they've done here, Le Kanak and his Countess? During their trial, they spoke of strips of human flesh... If they didn't eat them, what did they do with them?

(*As he examines the coat, a booklet falls from its pocket.*)

LA FICELLE: What's that? (*reading*) "Organ grafting. The Discoveries of Doctor Carrel." What does it mean? Here's a page annotated in Le Kanak's handwriting. "Why not experiment on humans with grafts which succeeded so well with animals?" (*with a cry of horror*) Could this be possible? Could Le Kanak have done it? Would Chéri-Bibi want this? Yes, he would! He would take his revenge that far!

(*Le Rouquin enters from the forest carrying a basket.*)

LE ROUQUIN: La Ficelle! La Ficelle!

(*La Ficelle appears in the doorway of the hut holding a picnic basket.*)

LE ROUQUIN: We're having lunching on board. Le Kanak asked me to bring you a basket. You must be hungry.

LA FICELLE: I'm not.

LE ROUQUIN: (*handing him the basket*) C'mon! There's some wonderful Spanish cod inside.

LA FICELLE: (*with a sad smile*) Chéri-Bibi loved Spanish cod. It was I who prepared it for him with my own hands. (*a pause, then abruptly*) I just had an idea. (*taking the basket*) Thanks, but I'd prefer to eat alone.

LE ROUQUIN: As you will.

(*Le Rouquin leaves. La Ficelle opens the basket and pulls out a plate of Spanish cod.*)

LA FICELLE: It smells of red peppers, thyme and laurel.

(*He positions the plate prominently on a chest.*)

LA FICELLE: If the Marquis comes back...

(*At this moment, Chéri-Bibi returns.*)

LA FICELLE: Here he is!

(*La Ficelle goes back inside the hut and hides behind the door. Chéri-Bibi steps forward, then stops suddenly. He expresses an uneasy joy as he smells the unexpected odor. He looks about, and, after a few hesitations, approaches the plate of fish on the chest. As he leans over it, La Ficelle appears in the doorway. Chéri-Bibi recoils abruptly.*)

LA FICELLE: The Marquis du Touchais hated Spanish cod.

CHÉRI-BIBI: (*stiffly*) Why, I don't know what you mean.

LA FICELLE: (after a pause) I have to impart some tragic news to Monsieur le Marquis. When I left France, Madame la Marquise, (*emphasizing his words*) your wife, was dying.

CHÉRI-BIBI: (*with a scream*) Cécily! Cécily is dying! Fatality!

LA FICELLE: (*delirious*) "Fatality!" He said it! He's betrayed himself! Ah, Chéri-Bibi! It's really you!

(*They throw themselves in each other's arms and embrace each other for a while.*)

CHÉRI-BIBI: But not a word! You know nothing.

LA FICELLE: So you are the Marquis du Touchais now?

CHÉRI-BIBI: Yes, my good La Ficelle. I have finally reached my goal. I am now Cécily's husband.

CURTAIN

SCENE V
THE STAR OF DIEPPE

A grand salon. In the back, there is a window-door leading onto a terrace. Beneath this terrace is a garden; in the distance, one can see the sea. On each side, there are two doors. The salon is comfortably furnished, mixing some old Normand furniture with some modern (1913) English style pieces. There are numerous knick-knacks and flowers in vases. It is 2 p.m.

AT RISE, Reine is reading to Petit Bernard; they are both seated at a small round table. Reine has aged greatly since the prologue. Petit Bernard is a lad of about six.

BERNARD: A, B, C...

REINE: That's very good, Bernard, continue.

BERNARD: D, da, dada...

REINE: Right. Dada.

BERNARD: Daddy. Say, Reine, where is Daddy?

REINE: (*unable to repress a violent start*) Your Daddy...
　　　　(*pause*) Don't ever speak of your father!

(*Cécily enters by a side door; her face is marked with sadness.*)

CÉCILY: The Dowager Marquise is not in her apartment?

REINE: Before lunch, Sister Mary of the Angels came for her and they went together to the Maritime Orphanage. I don't know if she's back yet.

CÉCILY: Would you find out, and if she is, ask her if she can see me.

REINE: Yes, Madame.

(*Reine leaves by a side door.*)

CÉCILY: (to Bernard who has not left his seat) Well, my darling, aren't you coming to hug your mother?

BERNARD: I'm studying my alphabet.

CÉCILY: How sweet he is, a studious little boy applying himself.

(*Bernard gets up and runs to his mother.*)

CÉCILY: You love me a lot, don't you?

BERNARD: Oh, yes!

(*Reine returns.*)

REINE: The Dowager Marquise has just returned; she's following me.

CÉCILY: Reine, take the boy to the beach. (*to Bernard*) Go play, my darling!

BERNARD: I want to fish for shrimps.

CÉCILY: Don't get too wet. (*to Reine*) Don't leave him alone for a single moment.

(*The Dowager Marquise du Touchais enters; she's nearly 60, but very alert; very well bred, a very grand manner.*)

MARQUISE: (*to Bernard, who's getting ready to leave with Reine*) Heavens! My dear, here's what Sister Mary of the Angels sent you. (*giving him a small package*)

BERNARD: (*opening it*) Chocolate! (*starts to eat immediately*)

CÉCILY: Bernard! You know how bad it is to be a glutton!

BERNARD: (*going to the Dowager Marquise and offering her some chocolate*) Sorry, Grand-Mother. (*going to Reine*) Reine (*going to Cécily*) Mama. (*a pause*) Can I take one now?

MARQUISE: Yes, my dear.

(*Bernard leaves, pulling Reine.*)

MARQUISE: You wanted to speak to me, Cécily?

CÉCILY: Yes, mother, I have bad news to confide to you.

MARQUISE: One more thing more to add to my painful life.

CÉCILY: We will endure it together.

MARQUISE: Our sorrows, having the same source, you can open your heart to me, child. It's a mother who is listening to you.

CÉCILY: You haven't failed to notice the frequent visits of Monsieur de Pont-Marie to this house?

MARQUISE: Yes! Being a friend of Maxime, George is trying to bring you some distractions from...

CÉCILY: No. What you and I initially mistook for friendship and compassion hides, in reality, another ignoble motive. Monsieur de Pont-Marie wants me to become his mistress.

MARQUISE: Impossible! Are you certain you're not mistaken about his intentions?

CÉCILY: Alas, no! If I was still capable of entertaining some illusions about Monsieur de Pont-Marie, his shameful behavior yesterday at the Casino would have shattered them all. So I'm afraid I'm going to have to forbid him to visit us in the future. I wanted to tell you my reasons, as you are my only defender, my husband no longer caring about my reputation.

MARQUISE: (*sadly*) Your husband. (*pause*) I am his mother. I would like to find excuses for him, but I cannot.

CÉCILY: After having paid his ransom on the *Bayard*, I said to myself, the trials he has endured must have softened him. Being a prisoner of convicts, isolated from society, he must have reflected, understood his villainy, he must have changed....

MARQUISE: Vain hopes!

CÉCILY: ...But once he regained freedom, he resumed his earlier life without even coming here, showing no more concern for his mother or his wife than if they were dead. He spends all his time with his new private secretary...

(*A servant enters.*)

SERVANT: (*to Cécily*) Monsieur de Pont-Marie begs Madame to receive him.

CÉCILY: See what I mean, mother? (*to the servant*) Wait.

MARQUISE: See him! I still want to think of him as a gallant man! I'll leave you.

(*The Marquise leaves by a side door after having embraced Cécily.*)

CÉCILY: (*to the servant*) Show him in.

(*The servant leaves, then returns with Monsieur de Pont-Marie, now fortyish, the rakish type.*)

CÉCILY: (*abruptly*) Why are you here, Monsieur? I thought that, after what happened between us before, you wouldn't dare to set foot here.

PONT-MARIE: I beg you to listen to me. You know very well that I am in love with you...

CÉCILY: I'd rather forget it. You gave me your word as a gentleman to not cross my door again, at least if you don't have the strength to remain an honest man, and hide feelings that can only outrage an honest woman! You swore to this two years ago.

PONT-MARIE: I did indeed, Madame.

CÉCILY: I thought you had forgotten your folly.

PONT-MARIE: At my age, one never forgets when one loves the way I love you. I knew you as a young girl, and I loved you already. Please allow me, I beg you, to plead my case!

CÉCILY: It would be pointless. I do not love you, and never will love you, and it is my duty to not listen to you any further. The first time, I forgave you. Before the threat of my door being closed to you forever, you demonstrated a sincere repentance, so that I took pity on you. I was so alone, so abandoned... You then displayed so much understanding and generosity that I began to fee some real sympathy for you; I couldn't help it. But after the incident of yesterday evening, you will understand that we must never see each other again.

PONT-MARIE: You cannot ask that of me! I cannot live without you. I love you like a madman.

CÉCILY: Good-bye, Monsieur!

PONT-MARIE: Listen! Yes, for two years, I didn't say one word of love to you. Yes, I had the strength to hide the trouble of my heart from you. But if I had this courage, it's precisely because I thought you would, at last, understand that I adored you, and that you take pity on my long abnegation, my respectful silence, and my silent passion! I said to myself that so much pain would eventually earn its reward, and that, someday, you would change your mind and...

CÉCILY: (*heading toward the door*) Please leave at once, Monsieur!

PONT-MARIE: (*barring her way*) No. I won't leave before showing the depth of my heart! Why won't you let me love you? Why don't you love me? You no longer have a husband...

CÉCILY: The Marquis du Touchais is my husband.

PONT-MARIE: More than a year has passed since his return. Has he called on you? Written to you? No. It's as if his wife no longer exists for him. Why should you be there for him then? You're no longer bound to this man. You no longer owe him anything. You are free, Cécily – and I love you.

CÉCILY: Let me pass, Monsieur or I will call the servants.

PONT-MARIE (*seizing her in his arms*) I love you! I love you, Cécily! Why are you fighting me? We could be so happy!

(*He pulls her to him, but she manages to disengage herself and runs to the terrace.*)

PONT-MARIE: Don't scream, please! It's in your interest. I have a grave thing to tell you. (*looking deeply into her eyes*) It's about your son.

CÉCILY: (*suddenly still*) What about my son?

PONT-MARIE: Calm down. (*coldly*) You know very well what I mean! (*goes to shut the door*) Let's talk, Cécily. You're wrong to treat me the way you do. I'm your friend; I'm devoted to you...

CÉCILY: You're a liar.

PONT-MARIE: Perhaps, but as my lies have failed, I shall now speak the truth. you, Cécily, are not an honest woman...

CÉCILY: What?!

PONT-MARIE: I repeat: you are not an honest woman. You cheated on Maxime.

CÉCILY: Coward! You're taking advantage of the fact I'm alone to insult me. Get out! Get out!

PONT-MARIE: I dare you to kick me out now. Come on! Ring for your servants and I will tell everyone that your son's father is not the Marquis du Touchais!

(*Cécily shivers then collapses into a chair.*)

PONT-MARIE: You are silent.

CÉCILY: What do you want me to say to such abomination?

PONT-MARIE: Big words! You would do better to be reasonable and listen to me. (*emphasizing his words*) Petit Bernard is the son of your cousin, Marcel Garavan, who died of a fever in New Orleans five years ago. Since Maxime was often traveling, you were able to deceive him about the birth date of the child, so he never suspected that he wasn't the father. All this is correct, Madame?

(*pause*) Since do not reply, I assume we are in agreement.

CÉCILY: (*breathlessly*) In agreement about what?

PONT-MARIE: About what I just told you. As for the rest, you must guess what I want for the price of my silence. After all, the poor Marquis must be kept ignorant of the truth. I shall now retire to let you reflect on the situation, Madame! (*bowing deeply and going to leave.*)

CÉCILY: I knew you were capable of anything, but this story is patently ridiculous. No one will believe a word of it.

PONT-MARIE: I think you are mistaken, Madame. I have proofs, irrefutable proofs, that I can show. But I only wish to protect you. Let's make peace, and as I understand that it's painful for you to see me in this house, here's what I propose: We will leave tomorrow for Paris, spend a few days there together, and return as marvelous friends.

CÉCILY: Never!

PONT-MARIE: You must consider my offer, Madame.

CÉCILY: I'd prefer to die.

PONT-MARIE: But that won't save your son from disgrace. You must think of the next Marquis du

Touchais. Come! I want your response right now.

(*The servant returns.*)

SERVANT: Madame, Monsieur le Marquis is here and asks if Madame can receive him.

CÉCILY: The Marquis?

SERVANT: The Marquis du Touchais, Madame. Your husband.

PONT-MARIE: (surprised) Maxime! Here? (*affecting delight*) The Marquis! What a nice surprise. Why, show him in. Isn't this his home after all?

(*The servant leaves.*)

PONT-MARIE: I'll come back for your reply this evening. We'll leave under some pretext or another. I'll make that my business.

CÉCILY: (*shouting*) Tell the Marquis that I went to find my son and that I will return in a moment.

(*She leaves precipitously. At the same moment, Chéri-Bibi – looking exactly like Maxime – enters, dressed elegantly, followed by La Ficelle, also properly attired. At the sight of de Pont-Marie, he is hardly able to hide a sneer.*)

PONT-MARIE (*rushing to him, hand extended*) Now, here's a surprise! You've finally decided to come here... (*pause*) What's wrong? You're not shaking hands with me?

CHÉRI-BIBI: (*presenting La Ficelle*) This is Monsieur Hilaire, my private secretary.

PONT-MARIE: Why, speak to me, Maxime! Tell me something. I find you completely changed, although I must say, the change becomes you; you have a superb bearing.

CHÉRI-BIBI: Listen, Monsieur de Pont-Marie...

PONT-MARIE: What! "Monsieur de Pont-Marie," not George? What's next, "Vicomte," like a servant? Why are you being so formal all of a sudden?

CHÉRI-BIBI: ...I need a favor.

PONT-MARIE: Of course! Anything! What is it you wish?

CHÉRI-BIBI: (*switching tones*) I want you to beat it.

PONT-MARIE: Maxime! Always the prankster! I recognize you there.

LA FICELLE: (*aside*) Lucky him.

CHÉRI-BIBI: (*back to being formal*) Please understand me. It's been a long time since I've seen Cécily. I'd rather see her alone–not in your presence.

PONT-MARIE: She just asked me to tell you that she was going to find Petit Bernard. But that's fine, of course. I shall leave you two. We will have plenty of opportunities to chat later. Good old Maxime! (*saluting La Ficelle*) Monsieur!

(He leaves.)

CHÉRI-BIBI (*watching him leave*) Now there's someone who won't be gathering much moss around here in the future! (*to La Ficelle*) Well, my good Hilaire, we're almost at the end of our tribulations.

LA FICELLE: Monsieur le Marquis must be very moved.

CHÉRI-BIBI: Yes, La Ficelle, Monsieur le Marquis is so moved that Monsieur le Marquis would like to get out of here in a hurry!

LA FICELLE: This is not the moment.

CHÉRI-BIBI: I know, but I'm fearful! I'm going to see Cécily, who's my wife, now–and I can't adjust to the idea.

LA FICELLE: Better do so quickly.

CHÉRI-BIBI: What was Pont-Marie doing here?...

LA FICELLE: Monsieur le Marquis is jealous now?

CHÉRI-BIBI: Well, let him dare return and he'll find out who he's really dealing with.

LA FICELLE: (*angry*) Ah, no, let's have none of that! (*going to him*) Calm down. Aren't you supposed to be the happiest of men? Don't do anything foolish now.

CHÉRI-BIBI: I can't help it! Seeing the old country again, all my memories have returned and my heart bleeds again. (*lowering his voice*) It's almost as if Chéri-Bibi wasn't dead...

LA FICELLE: And yet, Chéri-Bibi *is* dead—to the entire world—present company excepted, of course.

CHÉRI-BIBI: (*a pause*) Le Kanak and the Countess know the secret too.

LA FICELLE: But they were among the dead when the *Bayard* was sunk by the gunboat launched in pursuit of it, and, just as La Ficelle has become Monsieur Hilaire, Chéri-Bibi can now sleep in peace!

(*Chéri-Bibi remains pensive. La Ficelle heads toward the glass door leading to the terrace when he receives a shock.*)

LA FICELLE: Look outside! That nun!

CHÉRI-BIBI: (*looking with a shiver*) Sister Mary of the Angels–Jacqueline–my sister!

LA FICELLE: And that old lady on her arm...

CHÉRI-BIBI: It's the Dowager Marquise! Who's now my mother

(*At this moment, the door opens and Cécily enters.*)

CHÉRI-BIBI: (unable to control himself) Cécily! (*resuming his calm, to La Ficelle*) Please leave us, Monsieur Hilaire.

(*La Ficelle bows to Cécily and leaves.*)

CÉCILY: (*icy*) I went to fetch your son, Monsieur, but he hasn't yet returned from the beach where I sent him in Reine's company.

CHÉRI-BIBI: I will be happy to see him again soon. But, please, Madame, may I have your hand.

(*Cécily extends her hand to him.*)

CHÉRI-BIBI: Why are greeting me so coldly? Yes, I know, I've behaved very badly towards you in the past, but you are a good woman, and I you will take pity on me if I reform, Cécily...

CÉCILY: (*looking at him with astonishment*) It seems odd that you call me Cécily in a tone so different from the one you used in the past. You never once called me Cécily when we were alone before...

CHÉRI-BIBI: Yes, it's the first time I've used your name in such a fashion, but I pray you will now allow me to call you so. If that doesn't displeases you, it will give me great pleasure. Many things have changed since we last saw each other. I've lived through some terrible events...

CÉCILY: I learned of them through the newspapers–and your private secretary.

CHÉRI-BIBI: Ah, yes. I must thank you again for the speed with which you secured my ransom. I know that I ought to have written you before, but I didn't do it for the same reason that has kept me away for more than a year...

CÉCILY: As for me, your behavior has not particularly surprised me. I have grown used to your callousness. After all, you didn't hesitate to throw us out, your mother and I, from the Chateau du Touchais, in order to install your mistress there!

CHÉRI-BIBI: (*imploring*) Cécily!

CÉCILY: Well, this is home. You are the master here. Go, stay, do whatever you like, it's your business. I can do nothing about it. But, I beg you, behave yourself, in such a way that I

won't have to feel ashamed again. That's all I
ask of you.

(*The servant enters.*)

SERVANT: Monsieur le Baron Proskoff begs Monsieur
le Marquis to receive him.

CHÉRI-BIBI: I will see him.

(*The servant leaves.*)

CÉCILY: Don't make the Baron wait. He is, I believe,
one of your friends. (*a pause*) His wife, too,
if your friend–the so-called "Star of Dieppe."

(*She leaves.*)

CHÉRI-BIBI: (*alone*) I knew that Maxime had behaved
very badly towards Cécily, but not to this degree! Poor Cécily! If only I could speak to
you as my true self... (*a pause, then going to
ring*) But first, let me get rid of this baggage.

(*The servant ushers Baron Proskoff in.*)

PROSKOFF: (*entering with hand extended*) Well, Marquis! It's not nice not to tell us of your return.
De Pont-Marie just informed me of it. But we
can discuss his later...

CHÉRI-BIBI: (*cutting him off*) What do you want?

PROSKOFF: Always to the point, eh? De Pont-Marie told me you hadn't changed much! My dear Marquis, I am here to scold you. My wife and I wrote you at every turn, and you haven't even deigned to respond. Have we done anything to offend you? My poor little Sonia thought she was dying for such a long while that I decided to resume my friendship toward her.

CHÉRI-BIBI: You've taken your wife back? Well, keep her!

PROSKOFF: I don't understand.

CHÉRI-BIBI: Perhaps you don't wish to understand. (*a pause*) By the way, my dear Baron, coming here, I walked by the park of my Chateau, the where you live with your wife. I can't compliment you on its upkeep.

PROSKOFF: What do you mean?

CHÉRI-BIBI: This: Don't you know that a tenant is obligated to maintain a rental property? And keep in good order all the appliances and facilities provided by the landlord. I noted at the Chateau that the kennel was empty, the fountains dry, the lawn yellow; in short, such infractions would permit the owner to demand the cancellation of the lease.

PROSKOFF: (*bewildered*) Are you speaking seriously?

CHÉRI-BIBI: As seriously as any owner speaking to his tenant.

PROSKOFF: Since you choose to use this tone with me, my dear Maxime, I will reply to you that we have a term of nine years, renewable at the tenant's discretion. I will renew it, that's all.

CHÉRI-BIBI: Ah, but you seem to be unaware that the first and foremost reason for the cancellation of your lease–in addition to all the other transgressions I mentioned–is the non-payment of rent. Do you have any rent receipts?

BARON: Now, that is too much! You know quite well that you yourself refused to receive any money for the rent.

CHÉRI-BIBI: You may believe that, Monsieur! It might even be true. But, as you well know, I recently suffered from a bout of exotic fever which damaged my memory somewhat, and I don't recall anything about it. So unless you can present me with your receipts by this evening, you will be expelled tomorrow morning!

PROSKOFF: But what have we done to you?

CHÉRI-BIBI: What have you done to me? (*looks at him and bursts out laughing*) Ask your wife!

PROSKOFF: Oh, Monsieur le Marquis, you are not being like a friend–and a gentleman. In fact, if I may be so bold–you're being a boor. I'm sorry to be forced to express myself this way!

CHÉRI-BIBI: And you, Baron, are nothing but a gigolo. Enough pleasantries now. Go!

PROSKOFF: My Goodness! If I had expected to be received like this!

CHÉRI-BIBI: Pack your bags. Tomorrow, I intend to reclaim the castle of my ancestors. Goodbye, Baron!

(*The Baron leaves, stupefied.*)

CHÉRI-BIBI: Ah! That was some fine work! I'm sorry I can't see the face the "Star of Dieppe" will make when she hears the news. Cécily will be quite pleased.

(*La Ficelle returns.*)

CHÉRI-BIBI: If you knew how delighted I am, my good La Ficelle....

LA FICELLE: Hush! No La Ficelle here, especially right now. (*a pause*) I'm here to announce a visitor–Inspector Costaud from the Dieppe Police.

CHÉRI-BIBI: (*starting*) I'll be damned!

LA FICELLE: Yes, the same one who was your arresting officer eight years ago.

CHERI BIBI: He wants to speak to me?

LA FICELLE: Yes. He actually insisted on it.

CHÉRI-BIBI: The Devil! There's no way to put him off?

LA FICELLE: No.

CHÉRI-BIBI: In that case...

(*Chéri-Bibi rings for a servant; once the servant responds, he issues his instructions.*)

CHÉRI-BIBI: Show the Inspector in.

(*The servant leaves.*)

CHÉRI-BIBI: (*to La Ficelle*) Stay with me. There's no way to know how this will turn out.

(*Costaud enters. He hasn't changed much in eight years; he's just as self-important and cock-sure of himself.*)

COSTAUD: Good afternoon, Marquis.

CHÉRI-BIBI: You are...?

COSTAUD: Inspector Costaud.

CHÉRI-BIBI: What brings you here, Inspector?

COSTAUD: Excuse me for showing up here, Marquis, but when I learned of your return, I had to see you.

CHÉRI-BIBI: And for what reason, my dear Inspector?

COSTAUD: It's about Chéri-Bibi.

CHÉRI-BIBI: Chéri-Bibi? Isn't he dead?

COSTAUD: Are you quite sure of it?

LA FICELLE: (*aside*) What is he getting at?

COSTAUD: Marquis, I have read with great interest the account you gave to the newspapers. Until then, I didn't really believe in the death of that notorious bandit, but your testimony, as well as the return of Sister Mary of the Angels after her brother's death, finally convinced me that Chéri-Bibi had died on that far-off island. And yet, lately, I've been plagued by presentments that this formidable villain has managed to give us the slip again!

CHÉRI-BIBI: How could that be?

COSTAUD: I don't know, Marquis, but I just am no longer so sure about his death! Chéri-Bibi die of illness like just anyone else? Just when he was about to receive millions? No, no, that's not possible!

CHÉRI-BIBI: So you think Chéri-Bibi managed to escape again?

COSTAUD: I'm not prepared to go that far–yet! But it wouldn't surprise me! He played so many tricks on us before! Couldn't he have managed a last one? Are you certain of having seen his body, Marquis?

CHÉRI-BIBI: Yes, Inspector. I saw him dead, just as I see you living. (*pointing to La Ficelle*) My Secretary can attest to this.

COSTAUD: I must be sure, gentlemen, for I'm still persuaded that one, I will find myself face to face with Chéri-Bibi again.

LA FICELLE: (*aside*) He doesn't know how truly he speaks.

CHÉRI-BIBI: Let me ask you something, Inspector. Are you still certain that it was Chéri-Bibi who murdered Monsieur Bourrelier and my father?

COSTAUD: Absolutely!

CHÉRI-BIBI: What the man in the grey hat? Chéri-Bibi spoke to me at length about him when I was his prisoner.

COSTAUD: Just a fairy-tale. (*a pause*)

CHÉRI-BIBI: That's all you have to tell me, Inspector?

COSTAUD: Yes, Marquis. But if I ever have an indication regarding the resurrection of Chéri-Bibi, I will come to share it with you, right away.

CHÉRI-BIBI: (*ironic*) And you will be right in doing so. Inspector Costaud, I have the honor of saluting you.

(*Gesturing for La Ficelle to accompany Costaud; Costaud and La Ficelle leave.*)

CHÉRI-BIBI: Whew! That imbecile almost scared me!

(*Seeing Cécily appear on the terrace, he opens the glass door and calls.*)

CHÉRI-BIBI: Cécily!

CÉCILY: What do you want?

CHÉRI-BIBI: I wanted to thank you for what you've done for my mother. I've behaved so badly toward her so that I don't dare to present myself before her; but I beg you to tell her the happy news that, in a few days, she will be able to return to the Chateau and live there again for the rest of her days.

CÉCILY: (*astonished*) If what you are telling me is true, she will weep for joy. But does this mean that *she* is leaving the chateau?

CHÉRI-BIBI: Yes, *she* is.

CÉCILY: Ah!

CHÉRI-BIBI: To be clear: Baron and Baroness Proskoff are leaving the chateau because I am kicking them out.

CÉCILY: (*bitter*) Has the Star of Dieppe displeased her master?

CHÉRI-BIBI: No, Cécily. There's only one woman in this world who counts for me now. You.

(*The servant enters.*)

SERVANT: Baroness Proskoff begs Monsieur le Marquis to receive her.

CHÉRI-BIBI: I'm not here.

CÉCILY: (*low*) No, do see her. (to the servant) Ask the lady to wait for a moment.

(*The servant leaves.*)

CÉCILY: You just told me that henceforth, you will now devote yourself to me. I would like to believe you, but your past conduct make me somewhat skeptical...

CHÉRI-BIBI: What proof do you want me to give you.?

CÉCILY: Baroness Proskoff is waiting for you. Receive her. From the result of your conversation, I will learn if I can believe you. 'Till later.

(*Cécily leaves.*)

CHÉRI-BIBI: It's not going to take long. She did well to come, after all, the Star of Dieppe. (*he rings*)

(*The servant returns.*)

CHÉRI-BIBI: Show her in.

(*Sonia, Baroness Proskoff, enters, ushered in by the servant; she's thirtyish, very pretty, very elegant.*)

SONIA: Hello, my dear Maxime.

CHÉRI-BIBI: (cold) Good afternoon, Madame.

SONIA: Has my imbecile of a husband told me the truth? Your feelings about us have changed to this degree? (*she stares at him curiously touching his face with her hands*) It's strange, but when I look at you closely, I don't recognize you at all! From a distance, it's you, but up close, I doubt it! I know quite well that an illness can transform a man, but in your case, it seems to have improved you.

CHÉRI-BIBI: Madame, I prefer you not touching my face.

SONIA: And to think that I once satisfied all your whims... (*coming close to him*) Come on! Kiss your little Sonia, who still loves. (*Chéri-Bibi recoils*) My, my, you are really appalled!

CHÉRI-BIBI: Not here, in my wife's home!

SONIA: Now, there's a thing that you would have mocked before. Could you have made peace the little prude?

CHÉRI-BIBI: (*angry*) What did you call her?

SONIA: My God! Don't get so angry! There was a time when you wouldn't have gotten so vexed over such a trifle. So the Marquis returns to the conjugal bed! Hurrah! So much the better. Everything happens sooner or later in life! But, your reconciliation with your wife, my dear, doesn't excuse your rudeness towards me. At the very least, you ought to have replied to my letters, when I took such trouble to write them.

CHÉRI-BIBI: My private secretary opens all my mail, and didn't deem it useful to show them to me.

SONIA: You are joking, I hope?

CHÉRI-BIBI: Let's leave things as they are. That would be better for both of us–and for the one who plays the part of your husband.

SONIA: So be it! (*a pause*) Don't forget to present my respectful compliments to Madame la Marquise. Tell her that, in a few days, I will have the occasion to pay her a visit.

CHÉRI-BIBI: That's unnecessary, Madame.

SONIA: It's very necessary, for until I've paid her that visit, she will be unaware of the extent of her happiness, and that would be a shame.

CHÉRI-BIBI: What do you mean?

SONIA: I mean that, for her to appreciate the precious new virtue of her husband, she has to know his erstwhile unworthiness. Do you begin to see that my conversation may have its value?

CHÉRI-BIBI: I don't understand. What infamy are you plotting now?

SONIA: You treat me like a common harlot, I will avenge myself like one! I'll show her your letters!

CHÉRI-BIBI: As you please!

BARONESS: The letters you wrote me from *The Star of Dieppe* in which you promised to divorce Cécily in order to marry me.

CHÉRI-BIBI: So?

SONIA: ...And in which you made it clear that you were prepared to rid me of my husband by any means, in order to get me.

CHÉRI-BIBI: Witch!

BARONESS: And these promises are nothing compared to what you wrote about your wife. I'm sure that Cécily will be delighted to know how much you appreciated her, and discover how well you spoke of her. (*a pause*) A woman can forget everything, blows, infidelities, humiliations, but there are some things she will not pardon: the things that belittle her and hold her to ridicule.

CHERI-BIBI: I see. How much do you want for those letters?

BARONESS: My goodness! You are beginning to be reasonable at last! You were becoming uncouth, my dear Marquis. Don't you know that the gift is worth less than the manner in which it is given? Let's be like we were in the past, and I will deliver those letters to you. But you've got to behave properly again and be sweet to your little Sonia. If not...

(*Cécily returns and addresses Chéri-Bibi without acknowledging the presence of the Baroness.*)

CÉCILY: Maxime, I've just informed your mother of your decision regarding Chateau. She wants to see you right away! Come, so I can take you to her.

(*Chéri-Bibi remains still, looking desperate.*)

SONIA: As for me, Marquis, I want you to come with me to my chateau, which I am not going to abandon.

CÉCILY: (*to Chéri-Bibi*) Why aren't you kicking that woman out?

SONIA: Your arm, Marquis?

CHÉRI-BIBI: (*with a cry of despair*) Pardon, Cécily! Pardon!

(*He leaves like a madman, dragged by the Baroness.*)

CÉCILY: (*staggering*) This is horrible. He was making fun of me! He's betrayed me again!

(*She collapses into an armchair. Petit Bernard enters and, seeing her distress, he runs to her and clings to her knees.*)

BERNARD: Mama! Mama!

CURTAIN

SCENE VI
THE ABBEY OF THELEME

A large room in a very famous restaurant and cabaret. In the back, there is a large, open bay window, and a gallery about a meter high that leads to a restaurant that cannot be seen. At each extremity, there are two stair-cases parallel to the gallery that give access to the room. At the foot of the stairs, there are two large potted plants. On each side, there are two doors. On stage, there are couches, light tables. It is 2 a.m., but the lights are on.

AT RISE, a party is going full steam in the large hall; we hear shouting, laughter and fashionable music. Couples walk onto the gallery, men in evening dress, women in gowns. Then Chéri-Bibi and La Ficelle come down one of the stairs and quickly cross the gallery. They are dressed in evening clothes with coats. Chéri-Bibi addresses a waiter on duty at the foot of the stairs.

CHÉRI-BIBI: Ask if Baron Proskoff has reserved a table and if he has arrived.

WAITER: Yes, Monsieur!

(*The waiter leaves; Chéri-Bibi nervously surveys the room.*)

LA FICELLE: I beg you, calm down.

CHÉRI-BIBI: (*agitated*) That's easy for you to say.

LA FICELLE: Don't get yourself all worked up; you're going to attract attention. (*pointing to couples crossing the gallery*) Everything was going so well! And now, this evil Baroness is threatening all our beautiful work! It was all going like clock work, and suddenly–Boom! Nothing works any more; falls apart!

CHÉRI-BIBI: It's because of those damn letters. But she promised to give them to me. They have to come!

LA FICELLE: That poor Maxime sure had a passion for letter-writing; what joy!

CHÉRI-BIBI: I tell you, La Ficelle, I must have those letters!

(*The waiter returns.*)

WAITER: Baron Proskoff has indeed reserved a table, but he has not yet arrived.

CHÉRI-BIBI: Thanks.

LA FICELLE: Since you want those letters that much, why didn't you offer the Baroness a large sum of money?

CHÉRI-BIBI: What do you think? That was my first move.

LA FICELLE: And it didn't work?

CHÉRI-BIBI: No. When I think that Cécily was ready to forgive me, I mean Maxime, for his past misconduct, and that I had succeeded, through sheer persuasion, to defeat her antipathy towards me... And then, this accursed "Star of Dieppe" threw herself in my path! Ah, she'd better be careful that one, because if not...

LA FICELLE: Please, remember that we are not alone here.

CHÉRI-BIBI: Yes, yes, you're right, I must control myself! And this de Pont-Marie who's paid assiduous court to Cécily... What if, in order to avenge herself for this new insult, she threw herself into his arms? No, no, it's impossible! I will win Cécily's heart—or die.

LA FICELLE: What irony to bring such a cruel sorrow to this place of laughter and music. Who could have predicted, when I was mucking up sauces in the kitchens of the Chateau, that one day, I'd be going to the Monastery of Thélème in the company of the Marquis du Touchais?

(*Suddenly, Chéri-Bibi points out the Baron and Baroness Proskoff who have just entered the gallery.*)

CHÉRI-BIBI: There they are! Come on, amuse yourself, my good La Ficelle—since you can!

(La Ficelle leaves. The Baron and the Baroness enter the stage from the back having walked down the stairs.)

PROSKOFF: My apologies for having made you wait, Monsieur le Marquis. We've just come from a dress rehearsal of a show in Montmartre. The author of that little bit of obscenity is one of our friends. First of all, my dear Maxime, I must tell you how happy I am to resume our excellent relations. Yesterday, you said some unpleasant things to me–to which I paid little attention, truth be told. (*offering his hand*) I've forgotten them. Besides, the Baroness has told me how regretful you felt just after. So, let's speak no more about them. Let's all be happy!

(A Maître d' enters.)

MAITRE D': The gentlemen have reserved a table?

CHÉRI-BIBI: I was told there was one in the name of Baron Proskoff.

MAITRE D': Certainly. Would you like to give me your orders now?

SONIA: (*to Chéri-Bibi*) Pick the menu, my dear. (*low*) My tastes are yours.

MAITRE D': Monsieur le Marquis usually trusts me. Don't you remember me? I'm Henry, from the Cafe de Paris. I'm happy that Monsieur le Marquis has returned. (*low*) And even happier should Monsieur le Marquis remember that he owes me two hundred francs?

CHÉRI-BIBI: Right! (*quickly pulling out his wallet*) Here are three hundred.

MAITRE D': I am Monsieur le Marquis' most humble servant! The menu will be perfect

(*He leaves.*)

CHÉRI-BIBI: (*furious*) What an idiot! Borrowing money from servants!

SONIA: Of whom are you speaking, my dear?

CHÉRI-BIBI: Of an old friend whom I has instructed to pay my expenses and who was indelicate enough, as you have just witnessed, to leave me with debts everywhere.

SONIA: That's not too serious!

PROSKOFF: My dear Marquis, I've planned a little surprise for you. Imagine that among the interpreters of the show we just saw were Carmen de Fontainebleau and Nadja de Valrieu. I invited them to come to dine with us, and they accepted enthusiastically. The Baroness found the idea charming; I thought it wouldn't displease you either.

CHÉRI-BIBI: Indeed. The more fools there are...

SONIA: ...The merrier!

PROSKOFF: My dear, you must see Nadja dance the tango and hear Carmen sing a naughty little song! It's delightful! And then, they're charming company.

(*Nadja and Carmen enter at the rear.*)

PROSKOFF: Ah! Here they are! Come, Ladies, we were talking about you, saying bad things, of course! May I introduce you to my wife, the Baroness Proskoff.

NADJA AND CARMEN: (*with deep curtsies*) Baroness!

SONIA: Oh, please, no ceremonies for me.

CARMEN: Great! We're famous, you know?

NADJA: (*to Chéri-Bibi*) Hello, Maxime. You seem a bit healthier than you were on the *Bayard*.

CARMEN: (*to Chéri-Bibi*) You will come see our show? I play the orange.

NADJA: And I, a self-inflating tire.

SONIA: I'm sure these two young ladies display awesome talents.

PROSKOFF: Yes. Especially their legs.

(*At this moment, a boisterous Conga line passes on the gallery.*)

PROSKOFF: The Conga!

NADJA: Let's go!

PROSKOFF: Are you coming, Baroness?

SONIA: No, thank you.

PROSKOFF: What about you, Maxime? No? Then I entrust my wife to you; I know she'll be safe.

(*Holding hands, the Baron, Carmen and Nadja join the conga line passing through the gallery, then vanish.*)

SONIA: Well, Maxime! You were once a gay companion; now, you're positively lugubrious! If you didn't look the same, one would swear that you're a different man. You even look younger! But you seem to have lost that fine air of aristocratic nonchalance that made you laugh at everything. Now, it's almost as if some kind of cold blood ran in your veins. And you're restless, too. At this moment, you look pale–amazingly pale.

CHÉRI-BIBI: You think you can still hold on to me and play with me like a toy; but take care, Sonia! I will not always be in your power. Yesterday, I was weak enough to obey you. I offended my wife...

SONIA: The poor thing is used to it.

CHÉRI-BIBI: I might have created a chasm between she and I that I can no longer bridge. What more do you want?

SONIA: I already told you: a little kindness. For reasons I can't fathom, you've had enough of me. After having adored me–and you did adore me, darling!–it pleases you to repudiate me. I have too much dignity to force myself on you. Besides, I'm not your wife. But I want us to leave each other in a friendly way, with all the niceties that behoove people of our condition. You seem to have lost your good education in the company of these ruffians. In fact, my dear, if you don't mind my telling you, you are more like a convict than a Marquis now.

CHÉRI-BIBI: (*unable to repress a shiver*) Your reproaches touch me. I beg you to excuse my conduct. It is the result of the nervous condition I have developed since my unfortunate illness. Let's be reasonable, my dear. Will you return those letters you promised me?

SONIA: A promise is a promise. I'll be true to my word. You thought that Baroness Proskoff would exchange your peace of mind in return for money? I was insulted! You must understand that, since I can no longer have your love, that you've given to Cécily, I no longer ask anything from you but your friendship. If you still love me, even a little, then I'm sorry for you. Hearing this music, seeing these lights, smelling these flowers, might remind you of our amorous rendezvous? That might be your punishment, for make no mistake: these are things of the past now. I have invited you here to bury our love, not rekindle it.

CHÉRI-BIBI: Very well. So you will return those letters to me?

SONIA: I'm a better person than you think. I've decided to give them back to you tonight.

CHÉRI-BIBI: (*excitedly*) You have them on you?

SONIA: Souvenirs like that? Never! While my husband is getting drunk in pleasant company, let's dine in a private room together. That will be our good-byes, and I will give you these letters which you've taken so much to heart!

CHÉRI-BIBI: You're not still playing with me?

SONIA: I have only my word. Come!

(*Chéri-Bibi and the Baroness leave by a side door. La Ficelle enters from the bay window at back with a dancing girl named Toinette on his arm.*)

LA FICELLE: Oh! Paris! Paris! The women! If any virtue remains in me, I think that it will die tonight!

TOINETTE: Will you buy me a drink, honey?

LA FICELLE: My little kitten, I can't refuse you anything.

TOINETTE: Oh! Then we're going to get along fa-
mously! (*calling*) Hey, Maitre D'! (*nothing*)
How annoying! There's never a waiter when
you need one.

LA FICELLE: You want a beer?

TOINETTE: A beer? You must be joking! I want some
champagne. (pause) I like you a lot, you
know. You're handsome.

LA FICELLE: What's your name?

TOINETTE: Toinette!

LA FICELLE: Well, Toinette, I'm buying you a bottle
of the best champagne. (*aside*) There go my
savings!

(*La Ficelle and Toinette leave by a side door. The Baron
comes down the stairs supported by Nadja and Carmen.*)

PROSKOFF: (*drunk*) I tell you she's cheating on me.
I'm sure of it.

CARMEN: (*to Nadja*) He's drunk like a skunk.

NADJA: (*to Proskoff*) Who's cheating on you, dear?

PROSKOFF: (*weeping*) My wife, by Jove!

CARMEN: (*to Nadja*) There he goes again! Complaining to us about his wife's affairs!

NADJA: It's as if he only realizes he's a cuckold when he gets drunk.

PROSKOFF: (*tearful*) Where is she? I want to see her! I want to tell her what's in my heart. (*hiccups*)

NADJA: Hey, it's not as if she was having fun doing it!

PROSKOFF: Oh, my little Sonia! It's not nice! What about my family's honor! My reputation!

CARMEN: You don't have any, you old goat.

NADJA: Yes, shut up with your reputation!

(*Carmen and Nadja hoist him with difficulty up the stairs.*)

CARMEN: He must be tanked up to be so heavy.

(*La Ficelle and his dancing girl return, clinging to each other.*)

NADJA: Say, you two, give us a hand to hoist the load.

TOINETTE: (*to La Ficelle*) Come, little man, we gotta help the girls!

(*Chéri-Bibi enters and notices La Ficelle; he appears to be the prey to a great emotion.*)

CHÉRI-BIBI: Ah, it's you! Come here!

(*The Baron, carried by Carmen, Nadja, and Toinette, manages to get upstairs and vanish.*)

LA FICELLE: What's going on?

CHÉRI-BIBI: I let myself be dragged into a private dining-room with the Baroness to get the letters back...

LA FICELLE: And you have them?

CHÉRI-BIBI: Yes! But in the course of our conversation, it happened that this woman was able to see the tattoo on my breast which reads: "To Cécily forever, Chéri-Bibi."

LA FICELLE: Aie! Why did Le Kanak left that piece of skin on you?

CHÉRI-BIBI: Why? Why? I don't know! He had an odd sense of humor. It's too late to ask him now that he's dead.

LA FICELLE: Well, we're in for it for sure now! Are you sure she saw your name?

CHÉRI-BIBI: Yes, for she uttered a loud scream! She's discovered our secret!

(*Suddenly, he sees Cécily and de Pont-Marie enter dressed in evening clothes.*)

CHÉRI-BIBI: Them! Here!

(*Chéri-Bibi drags La Ficelle behind one of the large plants and hides while La Ficelle leaves without calling attention to himself. The Maître D' comes to greet Cécily and de Pont-Marie.*)

MAITRE D': Will the gentleman and the lady be dining with us? Would you like a private room? (*to a passing waiter*) Give them number 24!

CÉCILY: No thank you. I'll have a cold chicken wing in the main hall.

MAITRE D': (*bowing*) Very well, Madame!

(*He leaves.*)

PONT-MARIE: Then you stubbornly refuse to be alone with me?

CÉCILY: I agreed to eat something because I am tired You've been dragging me from cabaret to cabaret, trying to get me drunk.

PONT-MARIE: That's unfair, Cécily! I agreed to all your whims. Since we left Dieppe, you've arranged things so that we haven't had a minute alone! Must I actually insist that you honor the deal we made? No more words need to be exchanged between us? (*coming closer to her*)

CÉCILY: Don't come near me! Don't touch me!

PONT-MARIE: Why did you come then? There was no need for you to do so—unless, of course, you want to save your son! So I displease you as much as that? But don't be that way, let me love you. Until now, you've only seen me in an unfavorable light, but give me a chance and I can show you that I'm a gallant man and you will forgive me.

CÉCILY: (*pushing him away*) Yesterday, under the threat of infamous extortion, I was mad enough to agree to go out with you. I would have done much better to offer you money! All the money you wanted! All my fortune!

PONT-MARIE: Let's start all over again! Money! You know very well that I don't want it. If I needed any, your husband would give me some.

CÉCILY: To belong to a man like you—never!

PONT-MARIE: And yet, we deserve each other. Are you, perhaps, an honest woman? No! You're not. You've lied! You've always lied! You lied to your husband, to everyone else! You will be mine. You've had one lover; you can have another! (*smirking*) It's only the first one who counts!

167

(*He catches hold of her. At the same moment, Chéri-Bibi leaps from behind the plant where he was hidden and goes for Pont-Marie's throat.*)

PONT-MARIE: (*nearly strangled*) Help!

CÉCILY: (*fainting*) Maxime!

(*Chéri-Bibi releases de Pont-Marie who gets up as best he can.*)

CHÉRI-BIBI: (*terrible*) Get out of here! Now!

PONT-MARIE: (*waving his fist at him*) We will see each other again!

(*He leaves by the door at the rear making a final threatening gesture.*)

CHÉRI-BIBI: (*calmly looking at Cécily*) Do you want me to call for help?

CÉCILY: (*overwrought*) No! No one! I don't want anyone!

CHÉRI-BIBI: (*softly*) Then get hold of yourself, I beg you. Your pain makes me ill.

CÉCILY: After what you heard...

CHÉRI-BIBI: Yes, I heard everything.

CÉCILY: I am not imploring your pardon, and I take the entire responsibility for my sin! I married you purely out of filial duty. I didn't love you and you made no attempt to win my heart. During one of your trips with your habitual entourage of whores and gamblers, Marcel Garavan came. I loved him, and I granted him a joy that I would always have refused him, if, through your ignoble conduct, you hadn't given me every reason to do so! But I have been guilty! I've betrayed my duties as a spouse, and your honor as a husband ought to demand revenge! I await your decision. I've told you the story of my sin. Don't think I am trying to provoke your pity! But you made me suffer so much that I had an imperious need to shout out my suffering to you.

CHÉRI-BIBI: I'm the one who's guilty. The real culprit is me! I forgive you for everything. Don't be afraid, neither for yourself, nor for Petit Bernard, our son!

CÉCILY: (*incredulous*) Our son!

CHÉRI-BIBI: Yes! I will continue to love that child. He will continue to bear my name; he is innocent of a sin for which I do not have the bad to faith to blame you. When the Marquis du Touchais behaved in such a manner towards a wife such as you, he deserved all that and more.

CÉCILY: Perhaps, someday, you might regret your generosity?

CHÉRI-BIBI: No, Cécily, because I love you! And that love is so invincible that it can withstand crises which would doom other couples. We each had plenty of reasons to despise each other, but an innocent child came into this world, and those reasons have vanished. Cécily, I love you, and I defy you now to tell me that it is not reciprocated.

(*At the same moment, we hear a violent uproar. Diners erupt into the hall.*)

MAITRE D': This is too horrible! Shocking. (*to a waiter*) Go fetch the police at once!

CHÉRI-BIBI: What's wrong?

(*Inspector Costaud enters.*)

COSTAUD: They've just discovered the body of Baroness Proskoff in a private dining room. Strangled.

CÉCILY: The poor woman!

CHÉRI-BIBI: (*realizing*) Inspector?

COSTAUD: More than ever, I believe that Chéri-Bibi isn't dead. He is the murderer!

CURTAIN

SCENE VII
DOCTOR WALTER

At the Chateau du Touchais. The Boudoir of the Dowager Marquise. There is a door on each side. At the rear, French doors give access to a balcony. We sea the sea in the distance. It is 10 a.m.

AT RISE, the stage is empty, then a side door opens and a servant enters, introducing Cécily, dressed simply.

CÉCILY: Would you call Reine? I would like to talk to her before seeing the Marquise.

(*The servant goes to the door, opens it, and makes a sign. Reine enters as the servant leaves.*)

CÉCILY: Did the Marquise spend a good night?

REINE: She seems to be fine this morning, and if this improvement continues, the doctor will certainly authorize her to resume her usual walks.

CÉCILY: Did you ask her if she would see her son today?

REINE: (*in a strange tone*) She told me she would agree to it.

(*Chéri-Bibi enters holding Petit Bernard's hand. They are in beach costumes. The boy goes to Cécily and shows her the boat under his arm.*)

BERNARD: Look, Mama! The nice boat that Papa brought me from Dieppe.

CHÉRI-BIBI: Good morning, Reine. (*she recoils slightly*) What's wrong with you? Do I frighten you?

REINE: (*trembling*) I will go inform Madame la Marquise of your arrival.

(*She leaves.*)

CÉCILY: It looks like Reine isn't happy about your visit. Why would she have something against you, my friend?

CHÉRI-BIBI: I don't know. But I didn't behave well towards my mother and Reine is her faithful companion. So it's likely she doesn't keep me in her heart.

CÉCILY: I told her more than once that I would be happy if she joined me in my efforts to obtain your mother's forgiveness. But I got the impression that she's tried to undermine them.

(*Petit Bernard goes to play on the balcony.*)

CHÉRI-BIBI: Your perseverance has triumphed over the my mother's resistance, and Reine's doleful

influence–if your impressions are correct. Let
Reine think what she likes, it's not important! What matters is that you trust me and
have forgiven me.

(*The door opens and the Dowager Marquise enters.
Seeing Chéri-Bibi, she remains motionless. Chéri-Bibi
seems very troubled.*)

MARQUISE: (*gripped by great emotion*) Maxime!

CHÉRI-BIBI: (*aside*) Am I not about to commit some
kind of sacrilege?

(*Petit Bernard returns.*)

BERNARD: Papa! Why aren't you going to kiss
Grandma?

(*He takes Chéri-Bibi by the hand and leads him to the
Marquise.*)

MARQUISE: (*kissing Chéri-Bibi*) Maxime, my son!

CHÉRI-BIBI: Mother, I've done many wrongs to you,
but I undertake to use the rest of my life to
make you forget them.

MARQUISE: You've already begun, Maxime! Since
you let me return to our chateau.

CHÉRI-BIBI: I am ashamed of having made you leave
it.

MARQUISE: For a long time, I refused to see you, but then, I said to myself, I must embrace my son one last time.

CÉCILY: We are celebrating your return today.

MARQUISE: I don't feel very well, my dear child. I am a very old woman, and Maxime has returned too late. Nonetheless, I will not sadden this day that you are going to spend with me.

CHÉRI-BIBI: But, mother, you're still very healthy.

MARQUISE: Alas, that's not the opinion of my doctor.

CÉCILY: I saw him at your bedside and he made a good impression on me.

MARQUISE: Indeed, and I decided that you should meet him, so I begged him to come to lunch with us, with his wife whom he wants to introduce to me.

CÉCILY: (*to Chéri-Bibi*) Doctor Walter recently set up practice in the region and has quickly gained an excellent reputation.

BERNARD: Mama, can I go sail my boat on the lake?

CÉCILY: Ask your grand-mother, because you're at grandma's place.

MARQUISE: Certainly, my darling.

(*She pulls Bernard to her and kisses him. Cécily rings for a servant, who enters.*)

CÉCILY: (*to the servant*) Take the child to the lake and ask Reine to watch him.

SERVANT: Very well, Madame (*to the Dowager Marquise*) Doctor Walter has just arrived; I asked him to wait in the grand salon.

MARQUISE: Ask him to come up here, please.

SERVANT: Yes, Madame.

(*The servant leaves with Petit Bernard.*)

CHÉRI-BIBI: Take it easy, mother. I would be devastated if your strength betrayed you on the very day you welcomed me back.

(*The servant returns and announces:*)

SERVANT: Doctor Walter.

(*Doctor Walter enters–it is Le Kanak! He has hardly changed since the Bayard.*)

LE KANAK: (*going to the Marquise and doing a baisemain*) Madame la Marquise!

(*Chéri-Bibi stares at Le Kanak with horrified eyes, murmuring some unintelligible words, trembling, then leaning on a chair.*)

CÉCILY: What's wrong with you, Maxime?

(*She rushes to him and helps him sit in an armchair.*)

LE KANAK: (*naturally*) A slight dizziness, perhaps?

CÉCILY: (*to Chéri-Bibi*) Speak! You're scaring me.

CHÉRI-BIBI: (*regaining control of himself*) It's nothing. (*aside*) It's him!

LE KANAK: It must be the heat. It's very muggy this morning. Stretch out on this sofa. I'll examine you. (*pulling out a stethoscope.*)

CHÉRI-BIBI: (*stiffening*) No, thank you.

LE KANAK: (*going to the window and opening it*) Let's get some air in. (to the Marquise) Would you take my arm, Madame la Marquise, and walk in the park? I'm sure your son's malaise is only temporary.

MARQUISE: Is Madame Walter below?

LE KANAK: Indeed. My wife was very happy to accept your kind invitation.

CÉCILY: (*to Chéri-Bibi*) I'll stay with you.

CHÉRI-BIBI: No, really, I prefer to be alone for a minute. I feel much better already.

(*Le Kanak and the Dowager Marquise leave. Cécily follows them, after having placed a cushion under Chéri-Bibi's head. As soon as they are gone, Chéri-Bibi rises abruptly from the sofa.*)

CHÉRI-BIBI: Le Kanak! Alive! Such a striking resemblance! His bearing, his voice... It's really him!

(*A door opens and La Ficelle enters.*)

LA FICELLE: (*out of breath*) You're not going to believe me, but I just saw Petit-Bon-Dieu!

CHÉRI-BIBI: And I just saw Le Kanak!

LA FICELLE: (*shaking*) Him, too!

CHÉRI-BIBI: He's calling himself Doctor Walter now. Where did you see Petit-Bon-Dieu?

LA FICELLE: I was walking through the harbor when I saw him at the window of a winery.

CHÉRI-BIBI: Did he speak to you?

LA FICELLE: Yes. He told me that he'd fulfilled his life's dream and was at last established as a wine merchant and restaurateur.

CHÉRI-BIBI: He's working with Le Kanak! What are they trying to do? I'm cursed. Fatality! I understand now why he left that indelible mark on my breast. Ah! He's got me!

LA FICELLE:: You will defend yourself... We will defend ourselves!

CHÉRI-BIBI: I was so peaceful, so happy! Too happy! It couldn't last. (*a pause*) You really saw Petit-Bon-Dieu?

LA FICELLE: As I see you. And you are really sure it was Le Kanak?

CHÉRI-BIBI: Yes (*pause*) Heavens! Look!

(*Chéri-Bibi indicates with a gesture that La Ficelle should look outside.*)

CHÉRI-BIBI: The woman by his side who is speaking right now to Cécily...

LA FICELLE: It's the Countess! (*pause*) They're coming up the stairs. In a moment, they'll be here!

CHÉRI-BIBI: They didn't see you come in? *(negative gesture by La Ficelle)* In that case, get out of here.

LA FICELLE: But I could be useful...

CHÉRI-BIBI: It's better if Le Kanak doesn't suspect your presence.

LA FICELLE: Do you think he's going to try something against you?

CHÉRI-BIBI: His interest is to act carefully, at least for the moment. Come to my place this evening. I'll tell you what I've decided. Get going now, I hear them coming!

(*La Ficelle leaves. The Dowager Marquise, Cécily, Le Kanak and the Countess enter.*)

LE KANAK: Are you feeling better, Monsieur le Marquis?

CHÉRI-BIBI (*resuming his countenance*) Yes, thank you again.

KANAK: (pointing to the Countess) Allow me to introduce you Madame Walter, my wife, who's returned from a voyage overseas.

CHÉRI-BIBI (*with his old self-assurance*) Overseas, Madame?

COUNTESS: Yes. I was in India.

(*Cécily passes out glasses of Port which a servant brings on a platter.*)

CÉCILY: (*to Le Kanak*) Some Port?

LE KANAK: Thank you, Madame. (*to Chéri-Bibi*) But I understand that you've traveled greatly, too, Marquis. No one has forgotten the terrible story of the *Bayard* where you were taken prisoner by escaped convicts. I would love to hear you tell us your adventures.

CHÉRI-BIBI You must have read the details in the newspapers. They were full of them at the time.

LE KANAK: It is true that, after that brazen display of savagery, that awful Chéri-Bibi became somewhat of a celebrity.

CHÉRI-BIBI: Don't forget his accomplices, including one Le Kanak who particularly distinguished himself.

LE KANAK: Ah yes. They were some popular figures there. I believe there was a woman nick-named the Countess on board...

CHÉRI-BIBI Yes. She was Le Kanak's girl-friend.

LE KANAK: But they said she was in love with Chéri-Bibi, too. Was that true?

CHÉRI-BIBI: I wouldn't know. She didn't confide in me.

KANAK: (*abruptly*) Do you think Chéri-Bibi is really dead?

CHÉRI-BIBI: Yes, I do! Chéri-Bibi is dead! I myself saw his corpse thrown into the sea in a sack. His sister, a nun who lives nearby, was there, like me, at the sad funeral of this terrible bandit! He is dead! And I beg you to believe that he won't ever return.

CÉCILY: Why do you say that, my dear?

CHÉRI-BIBI: Because Doctor Walter seems to doubt my word.

(*Cécily goes to the balcony.*)

LE KANAK: It's just because Chéri-Bibi was such an extraordinary man that one can hardly imagine meeting an end that was so... trivial. Two years ago, I was vacationing in Dieppe when I had the luck to meet a certain Police Inspector.

CHÉRI-BIBI: You mean, Inspector Costaud?

LE KANAK: Yes, that's it. Well, Monsieur Costaud also didn't believe in Chéri-Bibi's death. It was futile to tell him what you just told us. He invariably replied: "Chéri-Bibi isn't dead! He just disappeared and, mark my words, you'll see that one day, he'll return under another name or another face." I recently met Inspector Costaud again, who told me: "I wasn't mistaken. I can still smell the presence of Chéri-Bibi in the air. The mysterious murder of Baroness Proskoff at the Abbey of Thélème is his work. I'm certain Chéri-Bibi will reappear on stage in the neighborhood of Dieppe. He'll be back." I will confess that his conviction amused me to the highest degree.

Can you imagine them arresting this bandit one night in the casino? If the Inspector is correct, Chéri-Bibi must have had the skill of impersonating a lord, a baron, a count–perhaps even a marquis!

CHÉRI-BIBI: You have a fertile imagination, Doctor.

MARQUISE: We will have to wait and see then. I feel warm. I'll go out on the balcony for a while.

(*She joins Cécily on the balcony.*)

CÉCILY: (*to the Dowager Marquise*) Here's the ferry from Newhaven pulling up to the pier.

(*Le Kanak joins Cécily and the Marquise. Chéri-Bibi approaches the Countess.*)

CHÉRI-BIBI: (*whispering*) Why are you here?

COUNTESS: To save you. Le Kanak and Petit-Bon-Dieu are plotting against you.

CHÉRI-BIBI: I suspected as much.

COUNTESS: Nothing is lost if you still love me a little.

CHÉRI-BIBI: (*ominously*) I can   rid myself of Le Kanak.

COUNTESS: I warn you, he has taken precautions. He wrote a will in which he revealed your true identity and gives proof of it.

CHÉRI-BIBI: Fatality! In that case, I can't harm him.

COUNTESS: That's why he's so confident.

CHÉRI-BIBI: But he got a million. How much more money can he want?

COUNTESS: It's not that. You are his masterpiece. He's not going to let you go–not after succeeding so brilliantly in reshaping your face. The million you gave him no longer matters; in fact, he lost it all in Monte Carlo, while he sent me away of a wild goose's chase in India. But I still love you, and intend to save you! Le Kanak's will is at Petit-Bon-Dieu's winery, in the room on the first floor, hidden in a desk in a corner. Steal it. Then you can decide if you want to rid yourself of Le Kanak.

(*The clock strikes noon. The Dowager Marquise, Cécily and Le Kanak return.*)

MARQUISE: Let's have lunch. (*to the Countess*) Allow me to show you the way, Madame.

(*The Dowager Marquise, supported by Cécily and followed by the Countess, heads toward the door that the servant has opened wide.*)

LE KANAK: I hope that the Marquise's appetite has returned.

CHÉRI-BIBI: As for the Marquis du Touchais, his appetite will be more than a match for that of Le Kanak.

LE KANAK: We shall see... Chéri-Bibi!

CURTAIN

SCENE VIII
THE WILL OF LE KANAK

The floor above Petit-Bon-Dieu's wine shop, located in a small street near the Dieppe harbor. It is night. The room seems sad Its only opening is a window at the back. On stage, there is a low table, some bottles, and in a corner an old desk.

AT RISE, Gueule-de-Bois and Le Rouquin are sleeping, their head resting on their arms, their elbows on the table. A lone candle stuck inside a bottle lights the stage. A moment passes, then a trapdoor opens in the floor revealing a staircase. Petit-Bon-Dieu enters, shuts the trapdoor and taps Gueule-de-Bois on the shoulder.

GUEULE-DE-BOIS: (*awakening with a start*) What's up! Oh, it's you, Petit-Bon-Dieu?

PETIT-BON-DIEU: Wake up Le Rouquin.

(*Wooden Throat shakes Le Rouquin, who responds only with groans.*)

PETIT-BON-DIEU: Come on, wake him up! This is not the time to snooze.

GUEULE-DE-BOIS: He's dead to the world. We must use force. (*leaning over Le Rouquin, he shouts in his ear*) The Police!

(*Le Rouquin awakens with a leap and, seeing Petit-Bon-Dieu and Gueule-de-Bois laughing at him, relaxes.*)

LE ROUQUIN: That was mean.

PETIT-BON-DIEU: Get up! It's time!

GUEULE-DE-BOIS: The time when honest men are in their beds. Will you finally tell us why you've gathered us here, Petit-Bon-Dieu?

LE ROUQUIN: He wants a house warming party. I've always loved parties.

PETIT-BON-DIEU: (*laconic*) It's about business.

GUEULE-DE-BOIS: What kind of business?

PETIT-BON-DIEU: You'll soon find out.

GUEULE-DE-BOIS: You're rather tongue-tied now that you're a wine merchant. They say wine makes the tongue wag; in your case, it deadens it.

LE ROUQUIN: As for me, I'm not curious. I don't give a damn whatever happens, so long as there's money in it.

PETIT-BON-DIEU: Well said, Le Rouquin. As for money, you can be certain there will be some–plenty.

LE ROUQUIN: Good! Because funds are rather low right now.

PETIT-BON-DIEU: What on Earth did you do with your share of the Marquis's millions?

GUEULE-DE-BOIS: Everybody's got his vice, Petit-Bon-Dieu. Yours was becoming a wine merchant, and you've prospered at it.

LE ROUQUIN: But the rest of us had millionaires' vices. For me, the whores. For Gueule-de-Bois, the races.

GUEULE-DE-BOIS: Enough of this! You promised us a nice job that would refloat all our boats. We're still waiting.

(*Several knocks are heard beneath the trapdoor.*)

PETIT-BON-DIEU: You wont have long to wait.

(*He raising the trapdoor and leans over the opening.*)

PETIT-BON-DIEU: Come on up, Doctor.

(*Le Kanak enters.*)

LE ROUQUIN: What a surprise!

GUEULE-DE-BOIS: Le Kanak!

LE KANAK: (*coldly*) Good evening! You're a bit surprised to see me, eh?

LE ROUQUIN: Not too much. The Devil and you, it's all the same.

LE KANAK: Time presses; let's talk (*low to Petit-Bon-Dieu*) Go keep watch.

(*Petit-Bon-Dieu goes to the window.*)

LE ROUQUIN: Go for it, Le Kanak! We're listening to you as if you were the Eternal Father himself.

LE KANAK: Here it is. I always thought that the sum of five millions was too small a ransom for a man as rich as the Marquis du Touchais, and that easily we could have obtained more...

LE ROUQUIN: For sure, since he was at our mercy.

GUEULE-DE-BOIS: If Chéri-Bibi only asked for five millions, he had his reasons.

LE KANAK: Reasons that he took with him to the bottom of the sea after he died in my arms. Still, I thought that Maxime du Touchais owed us an additional ransom, if only for the care I took of him during his illness. (*a pause*) Now, if you don't agree, I will settle this matter without you, for I have every intention of demanding a small supplement from him this very evening.

GUEULE-DE-BOIS: He's coming here?

LE KANAK: (*enigmatically*) He can't refuse anything to the doctor who saved his life.

LE ROUQUIN: He might not want to cough up more dough.

LE KANAK: Indeed. Fearing my eloquence alone might prove be insufficient, I thought that several of us could persuade him more easily.

GUEULE-DE-BOIS: I understood now.

LE ROUQUIN: It should be easy. As I recall, he was not very strong, that Maxime du Touchais.

LE KANAK: I'm afraid you're mistaken there. Since his illness, he's acquired a new vigor. I took such good care of him, you see... Four of us won't be too many. More are not necessary. The Marquis must simply be convinced.

GUEULE-DE-BOIS: I've always said it, Le Kanak. After Chéri-Bibi, you were the smartest of us all.

LE KANAK: Follow my orders to the letter and you won't have any reasons to complain. (*a pause*) I've set a trap for him. He may be suspicious and not come alone. (*pointing to the desk*) My bait is inside that desk.

PETIT-BON-DIEU (*at the window*): I hear a noise.

LE KANAK: (*going to the window*) It's him! Let's hide. I'll have plenty of time to give each of you my instructions.

(*Petit-Bon-Dieu, Gueule-de-Bois and Le Rouquin go down through the trapdoor. Le Kanak follows, after having blown out the candle. The room is plunged into darkness. A moment passes. Then, one sees light coming from the window. We hear the sound of glass breaking. A hand passes through the opening, opens the window and Chéri-Bibi climbs through. He moves his lantern around, then, seeing nothing suspect, makes a gesture. La Ficelle enters the same way. Both are wearing overcoats with the collars turned up, soft hats and kerchiefs around their faces.*)

CHÉRI-BIBI: (*examining the room*) No way out except through this trap door. Light up.

(*La Ficelle lights the candle.*)

CHÉRI-BIBI: (*pointing*) Here's the desk. Are you sure we weren't followed?

LA FICELLE: I've seen nothing suspicious.

CHÉRI-BIBI: Listen. No noise. We can't afford to be caught. If someone shows up, it will be his bad luck.

LA FICELLE: Yes, it would be indeed be regrettable if someone showed up.

CHÉRI-BIBI: You will do as I will, right, La Ficelle?

LA FICELLE: Since it's necessary, I won't hesitate. But I really hope we won't be reduced to that extreme.

CHÉRI-BIBI: I hope so too. Let's act fast. Everything must be done before dawn. Give me the crowbar.

(*Chéri-Bibi and La Ficelle head toward the desk.*)

CHÉRI-BIBI: (*breaking into the desk*) Poorly made furniture of no value. It won't take long. (*after another stroke, stronger than the first, the panel of the desk gives way.*) Where is the will? (*messes about*) Empty! The desk is empty!

LA FICELLE: (*pointing to a paper attached to the panel that was broken when the desk was forcefully opened.*) What about that piece of paper?

CHÉRI-BIBI: (*snatching the paper and reading it*) "Le Kanak presents his respectful compliments to the Marquis du Touchais and has the honor of informing him that he will not find his will here because it is kept in a safe place." We've been tricked. Retreat!

LA FICELLE: (*leaping to the window*) The ladder's no longer there!

CHÉRI-BIBI: It was a trap, a trap that the Countess baited for me, and I fell into it like a child.

LA FICELLE: What about that trapdoor?

CHÉRI-BIBI: Let's open it.

(*With the help of La Ficelle, Chéri-Bibi discreetly raises the trapdoor and both of them take a look below.*)

LA FICELLE: Le Kanak! Le Rouquin!

CHÉRI-BIBI: Petit-Bon-Dieu! Gueule-de-Bois! Our entire past is catching up with us.

LA FICELLE: They're ready to come up. What do we do, Chéri-Bibi?

CHÉRI-BIBI: We must protect the Marquis du Touchais. I'll throw myself on them. We'll roll onto the ground. You will have the advantage.

(*Chéri-Bibi opens the trapdoor wide, blows out the candle. In complete darkness, we hear the noise of a struggle, furniture being overturned, shouts, falling bodies, swear words, groans, etc, Then, the noise abates.*)

CHÉRI-BIBI: La Ficelle! My good La Ficelle..

LA FICELLE: Have no fear, I have nothing broken.

CHÉRI-BIBI: Give me some light.

(*La Ficelle scratches a match and lights a candle. Le Kanak, Le Rouquin, Petit-Bon-Dieu and Gueule-de-Bois are lying, unconscious, on the ground, in the midst of shattered furniture. In a corner, the Countess is dying.)*

CHÉRI-BIBI: (*with stupefaction*) The Countess?

LA FICELLE: What about the others?

CHÉRI-BIBI: We've been tricked again!

COUNTESS: (*in an expiring voice*) Don't think that I betrayed you. The proof is that I am dying for you. Wanting to save you, I almost destroyed you. Le Kanak tricked me. I know now where the will really is, it's with Monsieur Régis, the solicitor.

CHÉRI-BIBI: Thank you, Countess, you will be avenged.

COUNTESS: Chéri-Bibi! Come close, very close.

CHÉRI-BIBI: We'll get you out of here.

COUNTESS: It's not worth the trouble. It would hurt me too much. What's the use? I only ask one thing of you: kiss me. I'm waiting for this kiss before dying. I've committed many crimes in the past, but by saving you, I feel as if I'd gained a new soul. Ah, if only you had loved me! I could have done great things, but you couldn't do it, and now, evil horrifies me. I have only to die... (*she faints*)

LA FICELLE: Chéri-Bibi! Dawn is almost here.

CHÉRI-BIBI: We cannot leave her here!

COUNTESS: (*coming out*) Go away, Chéri-Bibi, go away. Kiss me, I have earned it.

(*Chéri-Bibi leans over the Countess and kisses her. She takes his head in her hands and clasps it, then her grasp loosens, her arms slide down. She is dead.*)

CHÉRI-BIBI: She's dead!

(*He stretches her gently on the ground.*)

LA FICELLE: Poor Countess! But we'd better go if we don't want to be caught by the police.

CHÉRI-BIBI: (*going to the window*) Too late. The police's here!

LA FICELLE: This time, there's no hope left!

CHÉRI-BIBI: Perhaps not. Give me your kerchief. (*placing the kerchief over La Ficelle's mouth like a gag; then, pointing to a bunch of ropes in a corner*) Now tie me up..

(*La Ficelle ties him.*)

CHÉRI-BIBI: Stretch yourself in a corner; I'll be in another. Now, we're ready for Inspector Costaud.

(*Chéri-Bibi stretches on the ground. La Ficelle, gagged, stretches out in another. A minute later, policemen leap through the window and come through the trapdoor, followed by Inspector Costaud.*)

COSTAUD: I arrest you all in the name of the law!

CHÉRI-BIBI: Help! Help!

COSTAUD: The Marquis du Touchais!

(*The police rush to untie Cheri-Bibi and La Ficelle.*)

CHÉRI-BIBI: I was lured into a trap with my secretary.

COSTAUD: I bet that it was Chéri-Bibi who played this dirty trick on you.

CHÉRI-BIBI: (*pointing to the Countess*) Chéri-Bibi himself, who would have done to us what he did to this poor woman if you hadn't arrived in time. Thank you, Inspector, thank you!

C U R T A I N

SCENE IX:
FATALITY

The office of the Marquis du Touchais. A vast hall with windows giving on the garden. It's the middle of the afternoon.

AT RISE, the stage is empty; then a door opens; Chéri-Bibi enters followed by a servant.

CHÉRI-BIBI: (*ridding himself of his hat*) Is my secretary here?

SERVANT: Following your instructions, I asked him to wait.

CHÉRI-BIBI: Please tell him that I have to speak to him right away.

(*The servant bows and leaves. Chéri-Bibi sits at his desk, then La Ficelle enters.*)

LA FICELLE: Did it all go well?

CHÉRI-BIBI Yes, more or less. I told Costaud to show the greatest discretion about last night's incident in order to not frighten the Marquise. Besides, Cécily will have other matters on her mind soon. I was called to the Chateau because the condition of the Dowager Marquise–my mother–has suddenly worsened. I has the unpleasant surprise to find that the so-called "Doctor Walter" had preceded me to her bedside.

LA FICELLE: Le Kanak is pushing audacity a little far!

CHÉRI-BIBI: Especially since he no longer has any hold on me, now that I've gotten his famous will is in my possession.

LA FICELLE: You were able to get hold of it?

CHÉRI-BIBI: Yes. When I left you after the interrogation that Costaud made us submit to, I managed to go cross country to the house of Monsieur Regina and there, wearing a mask, under threat of death, I made him give me the will.

LA FICELLE: But he's going to complain and Le Kanak will learn that his will has disappeared.

CHÉRI-BIBI: No, because I warned him that he would be exposing himself to terrible reprisals on the part of Chéri-Bibi.

LA FICELLE: Then, we can breathe a bit easier. After the experience of last night, I doubt that Le Kanak will try again soon.

CHÉRI-BIBI: But I will not endure his perpetual threat. I promised the dying Countess to avenge her, and I will! It would seem that our adventures aren't quite over yet. Since I've taken on the identity of the Marquis du Touchais, I've ne-

glected Chéri-Bibi. I must now try to rehabilitate his memory, for the real murderer of
Monsieur Bourrelier and the late Marquis–
the man in the gray hat whom I saw–is still at
large.

LA FICELLE: We've faced so many terrible threats that
I'm not happy to hear you talk about facing
new ones. To rehabilitate Chéri-Bibi is a task
beyond human strength. (*a pause*) What is
your life's dream? To be loved by Cécily.
You've succeeded. What more do you wish?

CHÉRI-BIBI: You can't understand the joy I will feel
the day I hear : "You know this Chéri-Bibi,
the man they accused of so many crimes?
Well, he was innocent!" Because, you know,
my good La Ficelle, that I am not guilty. The
only crime I committed was the murder of
Baroness Proskoff, but I had no choice: it
was either kill her or lose Cécily. I decided to
keep the only woman I ever loved!

LA FICELLE: Order, Chéri-Bibi, and I will obey, even
if it proves fatal for both us. Such is my destiny.

CHÉRI-BIBI: Then, find Sister Mary of the Angels. Tell
her that you know someone who is taking an
interest in reopening Chéri-Bibi's case because of the recent commotion about him.
Add that this person has heard of Reine's
statements regarding Chéri-Bibi's innocence,
and that they feel that the moment has come

for her to tell the truth, and unmask the real murderer. The Dowager Marquise's agony must be very painful for Reine and it might help convince her to talk.

(*The servant returns.*)

SERVANT: Inspector Costaud asks if you can receive him now, Monsieur le Marquis.

(*The servant leaves.*)

CHÉRI-BIBI He's never arrived in so timely a manner. Quick! Go find Sister Mary, and take her to the Chateau so she can obtain Reine's confession.

LA FICELLE: Ah! Why do I feel that today is not going to be a peaceful day.

(*La Ficelle leaves as the servant returns with Costaud.*)

COSTAUD: Have you recovered from the emotions of last night, Marquis?

CHÉRI-BIBI Completely, Inspector, but without you, I was a dead man. It was a close call!

COSTAUD: I was busy this morning looking for Chéri-Bibi. All the trails end here or at the Chateau. I think that this bandit is scheming to take you or your wife hostage again. So my men will not leave you, and I've had all the entrances and exits watched.

CHÉRI-BIBI I can only be grateful for your zeal, Inspector. Still, in order to not terrify my family, I would like your surveillance to be performed with the utmost discretion.

COSTAUD: Of course, Marquis. You can count on us.

CHÉRI-BIBI Tell me, Inspector. Are you still certain of Chéri-Bibi's guilt in all the original crimes of which he was accused?

COSTAUD: Certainly. When the police catch someone, it's always the guilty party.

CHÉRI-BIBI A terrifying logic. So much that I hesitate to share some personal thoughts with you.

COSTAUD: Monsieur le Marquis must be joking! I am always delighted and flattered to hear your thoughts.

CHÉRI-BIBI: When I was on the Bayard, I had numerous conversations with Chéri-Bibi, and he always protested his innocence of the murders of Monsieur Bourrelier and the old Marquis du Touchais, my father.

COSTAUD: ...And recounted to you for the millionth time his fantastic story of a man with a grey hat. That's all rubbish.

CHÉRI-BIBI: It's precisely on that very point, Inspector, that you and I are not in completely agreement. I inherited from my ancestors a stubborn streak and I got it into my head to find the man in the grey hat.

COSTAUD: (*laughing*) It's a distraction like any other.

CHÉRI-BIBI: But I did find him.

COSTAUD: (*stupefied*) What do you mean?

CHÉRI-BIBI: My goodness! You're no longer laughing, Inspector.

COSTAUD: Should I take you seriously, Marquis?

CHÉRI-BIBI: If I didn't have the pleasure of your visit, Inspector, I would have sent for you, because, within an hour, I will deliver to you the real murderer of the Marquis du Touchais and Monsieur Bourrelier. I don't know his name yet, but I can affirm that it is not Chéri-Bibi.

(*The servant returns.*)

SERVANT: Monsieur de Pont-Marie is here.

CHÉRI-BIBI: Ask him to wait for a minute and beg my wife to come right away.

(*The servant starts to go.*)

CHÉRI-BIBI: And let me known when Monsieur Hilaire has returned.

(*The servant leaves.*)

CHÉRI-BIBI: (*to Costaud*) Don't go very. I'm going to keep my promise.

COSTAUD: Marquis, you see me flabbergasted. Chéri-Bibi innocent? That really would take the cake!

(*Costaud leaves. Chéri-Bibi remains alone for a moment, then Cécily enters.*)

CÉCILY: You asked for me, darling?

CHÉRI-BIBI: I wanted you to read a letter which I just received.

CÉCILY: (*taking the letter and reading it*) "My dear Maxime, I behaved like a wretch, but I've been able to finally realize the enormity of my mistake and I am really repentant. I beg you to allow me to beg for Cécily's forgiveness in person. I hope that, after what happened between us, we can still remain friends. De Pont-Marie."

CHÉRI-BIBI: He's here and asks to see you in order to apologize to you in person. (*after a pause*) So be it!

(*To a servant after ringing a bell.*)

CHÉRI-BIBI: Show Monsieur de Pont-Marie in.

(*De Pont-Marie enters, introduced by the servant.*)

PONT-MARIE: (*to Cécily*) I realize how much my presence may revive some awful memories, Madame, but having decided to go away for a while, it was hard for me to leave without first asking for your pardon. And without being reconciled with Maxime.

CÉCILY: Since we shall no longer see each other, I pardon you for whatever offense you may have given me.

CHÉRI-BIBI: (*to de Pont-Marie*) You've decided to go away and have no intention of ever returning?

PONT-MARIE: Yes, and I'd like to talk to you about my plans.

CÉCILY: May I go now, darling? I must return to your mother's bedside.

CHÉRI-BIBI: Of course.

PONT-MARIE: (*bowing deferentially*) Madame.

(*She leaves as the servant returns.*)

SERVANT: Monsieur Hilaire is back and urgently asks to speak with Monsieur le Marquis.

(*La Ficelle enters.*)

LA FICELLE: (*to Chéri-Bibi*) I've brought Reine back with me.

CHÉRI-BIBI: Sister Mary of the Angels convinced her to talk? Excellent! At last, we'll know the truth. Take her to see Costaud; he will receive her confession. I must have a final word with de Pont-Marie.

(*La Ficelle leaves.*)

CHÉRI-BIBI: (*to de Pont-Marie*) I am listening.

PONT-MARIE: I've decided to go into exile and make a new life for myself far from here, but I need money to do that and I haven't got any. Give me a small stipend, say, a hundred thousand francs, very little for a man with your fortune, and you will never hear from me again.

CHÉRI-BIBI: You've already tried to take my wife, and now you're trying to take my money! You're either mad or cynical beyond belief!

PONT-MARIE: Let's not be angry, my dear Maxime. Notice how politely I have asked you to give me money, money which I could rightfully demand. When you half-strangled me at the Abbey of Thélème, and I went without causing a scandal, it was because I thought it was in our mutual interest not to have a public fight. But here, alone, face to face, I can tell you that if you have forgotten the past, I haven't.

CHÉRI-BIBI: I know you are capable of all kinds of blackmail, but I am not afraid of you.

PONT-MARIE: You don't lack courage, I'll say that for you! But stop posturing, Maxime, and listen to me. You have to stand by me since we both have blood on our hands.

CHÉRI-BIBI: (*startled*) Blood!

PONT-MARIE: Yes, blood! You know perfectly well what I'm talking about! What is this comedy? You won't get away with trying to intimidate me. I need money, so you'll give me some! And hurry up about it! Or you'll find that you've made a far costlier mistake. Remember when you were up to your neck in debt, like me, and needed cash in a hurry? That night, you told me "Monsieur Bourrelier will be carrying a hefty sum of money on his way back from Dieppe." It was at your behest that I attacked him on the cliff.

CHÉRI-BIBI: (*recoiling, haggard*) You're the man with the grey hat!

PONT-MARIE: And remember our rage when we discovered that the old man's wallet contained only a trifle sum compared with what we expected. Then, you said to me, "There's only one thing left for us to do: rob my father."

CHÉRI-BIBI: (*wheezing*) You're lying.

PONT-MARIE: Remember how your father surprised us in the middle of the burglary, and I thought that you were going to strangle each other. Remember how I forced him to let you go, just in time.

CHÉRI-BIBI: (*rasping*) You're lying! You must be lying!

PONT-MARIE: (*unstoppable*) At last, remember how your teeth were chattering as you hid me under the bed in your own room while we heard the commotion and saw the police arrest Chéri-Bibi, which, thanks to the Devil, saved our bacon! (*pause*) What's the matter with you? You look pale as a sheet.

CHÉRI-BIBI: (*gripped by a terrible emotion*) Fatality! I took on the face of what I thought was a honest man only to discover that he is a murderer! (*to de Pont-Marie*) Shut up! Shut-up!

PONT-MARIE: Have I ever spoken of it? Don't I have, just as you do, a vested interest in keeping the whole matter under wraps? No one must ever suspect us. No one knows a thing.

CHÉRI-BIBI: That's where you're mistaken! There is someone who knows! Someone who's come to denounce you; someone I brought here myself, who is speaking to Inspector Costaud at this very moment, and is giving your description to the police who are surrounding this villa.

(*Suddenly, Costaud enters, followed by several policemen.*)

COSTAUD: Monsieur le Marquis, you promised to reveal to me the name of the true murderer of the Marquis du Touchais and Monsieur Bourrelier. At your behest, the companion of the Dowager Marquise has come to make a confession, one that is so astonishing that I ask myself if the Dowager Marquise's death, which occurred just as the lady in question was leaving the chateau, did not disturb her sanity. Yet, this woman insists that she has irrefutable proof, which she will produce. So, I am now obliged to confront you with the lady...

(*He goes to the door, opens it. Reine enters.*)

COSTAUD: Madame, you have just made an accusation of such gravity that I fear that you may not have fully grasped its significance. Please remain calm. Here are Monsieur le Marquis du Touchais and Monsieur de Pont-Marie. Do you persist in accusing them of the murders of the old Marquis du Touchais and Monsieur Bourrelier?

REINE: Yes. I told the truth. (*to Chéri-Bibi*) I remained silent until now so that your mother would live, because I knew the truth would kill her, and I had such veneration for her that I wanted to preserve the peace and honor of her old age. So I knowingly allowed an innocent man to be condemned in your place, which was evil. But the hour of expiation has come with the death of the Dowager Marquise, and I am now handing the true murderers over to justice.

(*Chéri-Bibi remains annihilated.*)

PONT-MARIE: (*forcing himself to put on a brave show*) Inspector, I hope you're not going to give credence to the ravings of a senile old crone. Let her provide some evidence.

REINE: Here it is! (*pulling a wallet from her corsage*) This wallet was Monsieur Bourrelier's! The assassins stole it from him that very same day. I found it the following day under the bed of the young Marquis.

PONT-MARIE: (*uttering a muffled curse*) Bourrelier's billfold! We're lost!

COSTAUUD: What do have you to say on your behalf?

CHÉRI-BIBI: (*choking*) The proof Reine brought is sufficient. I will not oppose any resistance, but I beg you to fetch Doctor Walter immediately. I have revelations to make of the greatest importance, which I can only do in his presence.

(*Costaud signals to one of the gendarmes who leaves. Then he signals to two others.*)

COSTAUD: Take Monsieur de Pont-Marie away.

PONT-MARIE: (*as he passes Chéri-Bibi*) Time to pay the piper, Maxime, old boy.

(*He leaves in the custody of the gendarmes.*)

COSTAUD: Out of respect for your title I won't put the cuffs on you, but I'm keeping you under close watch.

(*La Ficelle enters and rushes to Chéri-Bibi.*)

LA FICELLE: What's going on? What is it that they told me? Can it be true?

CHÉRI-BIBI: Yes, La Ficelle, I'm a murderer.

LA FICELLE: You–the Marquis?

CHÉRI-BIBI: Good La Ficelle! The brave companion of my adventures! There's nothing left to do, except to finish the last act written for me by Fate. I sought to prove Chéri-Bibi innocent of the murder of the Marquis du Touchais, but you know who the assassin was? It's I, the old Marquis' own son! And now, I'm thinking of Cécily, whose heart I had finally gained! Fate is too unjust, La Ficelle, for I'm paying not only for the living, but for the dead But I do have one last act of vengeance to fulfill.

(*Le Kanak enters, preceded by a gendarme; seeing Chéri-Bibi, he looks worried.*)

COSTAUD: (*to Le Kanak*) Doctor, I sent for you because the Marquis du Touchais requested your presence when he makes his statement.

CHÉRI-BIBI: (*to Costaud*) You never believed in the death of Chéri-Bibi? You were right, Inspector. For I am Chéri-Bibi. Ask Doctor Walter.

LE KANAK: This man is mad!

CHÉRI-BIBI: Come on, "Doctor," take off the mask. The moment has come for you, too, to pay for your crimes. You will recollect Inspector, that a doctor was once convicted for carving up human flesh? That doctor was Le Kanak, and Le Kanak is Doctor Walter.

LE KANAK: That's false!

CHÉRI-BIBI: Taking advantage from the fortuitous presence of Maxime du Touchais aboard the *Bayard*, he grafted on me, Chéri-Bibi, the face of Marquis. The real Marquis died and was buried at sea under my name. The graft was so well done that, before you, stands Chéri-Bibi with the face of the Marquis du Touchais.

LE KANAK: Prove it!

CHÉRI-BIBI: (*pulling a sealed envelope from his pocket and handing it to Costaud*) Here's the last will and testament of Le Kanak himself, known to you as Doctor Walter, written in his own hand.

LE KANAK: Very well. Justice will have to determine if my discovery of skin grafting is a crime, and if a scientist can be compared to a murderer.

CHÉRI-BIBI: Are you a scientist? What use did you make of your discovery? You sought to make a docile tool of me, turn me into a puppet whose strings you could wield at your pleasure. Since fate decrees that I fall, I am dragging you with me.

COSTAUD: (*to Le Kanak*) In the name of the law, I arrest you.

KANAK: I'll follow you. (*passing by Chéri-Bibi*) You've just avenged the Countess.

CÉCILY: (*running in from the opposite door*) Maxime!

CHÉRI-BIBI: Don't approach me, Madame. I am one of those accursed souls whom fate pursues like a bird of prey. Whatever I may be, whatever I may do, whatever I may attempt, whenever I undertake to free myself from its yoke, I still find myself entwined again in the strands of

211

merciless fate, which always casts me back into the Hell for which I was born. Leave me alone. I must no longer exist for you. You were my only reason to live. Losing you, I will die, and rid the world of a monster whose soul is now trapped in a body that is not his. Goodbye, Cécily, Goodbye!

(*He leaves like a madman followed by Costaud and the gendarmes. Cécily has fallen into an armchair. La Ficelle weeps silently. Reine, her eyes haggard, remains still in a corner. Sister Mary of the Angels enters and heads slowly towards Cécily. She leads Petit Bernard by the hand.*)

SISTER MARY: Have courage, sister. Think of your son, and pray to God in whose heart resides pardon and mercy.

REINE: I wanted to save Chéri-Bibi and I am the one who destroyed him.

LA FICELLE: (*in a burst of tears*) Fatality!

CURTAIN

Bibliography of Gaston Leroux
(1868-1927)

1. L'Homme de la Nuit [*A Man in the Night*] (novel) (*Le Matin*, Dec. 5, 1897-March 14, 1898; Fayard, 1911)

2. Sur mon Chemin [*On My Path*] (collection of articles) (Flammarion, 1901)

3. La Double Vie de Theophraste Longuet [*The Double Life of Theophraste Longuet*] (novel) (*Le Matin*, Oct. 5-Nov. 22, 1903; rev. Flamm., 1904)

4. Les Héros de Chemulpo [*The Heroes of Chemulpo*] (collection of articles) (Juven, 1904)

5. Baïouchki Baïou (short story) (*Le Matin*, Jan. 2, 1907)

6. La Maison des Juges [*The House of Judges*] (stage play) (Odéon, Jan. 26, 1907)

7. Le Mystère de la Chambre Jaune [*The Mystery of the Yellow Room*] (novel; Rouletabille #1) (*L'Illustration*, Sept. 7-Nov. 30, 1907; rev. Lafitte, 1908)

8. L'Homme qui a vu le Diable [*The Man Who Saw the Devil*] (short story) (*Je Sais Tout*, Mar. 15, 1908)

9. Le Parfum de la Dame en Noir [*The Scent of the Lady in Black*] (novel; Rouletabille #2) (*L'Illustration*, Sept. 26, 1908-Jan. 2, 1909; rev. Lafitte, 1909)

10. Le Roi Mystère [*King Mystery*] (novel) (*Le Matin*, Oct. 24, 1908-Feb. 9, 1909; rev. Fayard, 1910)

11. Le Lys [*The Lily*] (stage play) (Vaudeville, Dec. 18, 1908)

12. Le Fauteuil Hanté [*The Haunted Chair*] (novel) (*Je Sais Tout*, Nov. 1909-Apr. 1910; rev. Lafitte, 1911)

13. Le Fantôme de l'Opéra [*The Phantom of the Opera*] (novel) (*Le Gaulois*, Sept. 23, 1909-Jan. 8, 1910; rev. Lafitte, 1910)

14. La Reine du Sabbat [*The Queen of the Sabbath*] (novel) (*Le Matin*, Aug. 18, 1910-Jan. 31, 1911; rev. Fayard, 1913)

15. Le Dîner des Bustes [*The Dinner of Busts*] (short story) (*Excelsior*, Jan. 29-Feb. 2, 1911)

16. Balaoo (novel) (*Le Matin*, Oct. 9-Dec. 18, 1911; rev. Tallandier, 1912)

17. La Hache d'Or [*The Golden Axe*] (short story) (*Touche à Tout*, Feb. 1912)

18. Le Mystère de la Chambre Jaune (stage play adaptation) (*L'Ambigu*, Feb. 14, 1912)

19. L'Epouse du Soleil [*The Bride of the Sun*] (novel) (*Je Sais Tout*, Mar.-Aug. 1922; rev. Laffite, 1913)

20. Rouletabille chez le Tsar [*Rouletabille and the Tsar*] (novel; Rouletabille #3) (*L'Illustration*, Aug. 3-Oct. 19, 1912; Lafitte, 1913)

21. L'Homme qui a vu le Diable (stage play adaptation) (*Grand-Guignol*, Dec. 7, 1911)

22. Alsace (stage play) (Réjane, Jan. 10, 1913)

23. Chéri-Bibi (novel; Chéri-Bibi #1) (*Le Matin*, Apr. 7-Aug. 4, 1913; rev. 2 vols. as Les Cages Flottantes [*The Floating Cages*] and Chéri-Bibi et Cécily, Fayard, 1914)

24. Rouletabille à la Guerre [*Rouletabille At War*] (novel; Rouletabille #4) (*Le Matin*, Mar. 28-Aug. 2, Oct. 18-24, 1914; rev. 2 vols. as Le Château Noir [*The Black Castle*] and Les Etranges Noces de Rouletabille [*The Strange Wedding of Rouletabille*], Lafitte, 1916)

25. Confitou (novel) (*Le Flambeau*, Dec. 4, 1915-Jan. 8, 1916; *Le Matin*, Jan. 16-Feb. 15, 1916; rev. Lafitte, 1917)

26. La Colonne Infernale [*The Infernal Column*] (novel) (*Le Matin*, Apr. 29-Sept. 8, 1916; rev. 2 vols. as La Colonne Infernale [*The Infernal Column*] and La Terrible Aventure [*The Dreadful Adventure*], Fayard, 1917)

27. L'Homme Qui Revient de Loin [*The Man Who Returned From Afar*] (novel) (*Je Sais Tout*, Jun. 1916-Jan. 17; rev. Lafitte, 1917)

28. Rouletabille Chez Krupp [*Rouletabille At Krupp's*] (novel; Rouletabille #5) (*Je Sais Tout*, Sept. 1917-Mar. 1918; rev. Lafitte, 1920)

29. Les Aventures Effroyables de Herbert de Renich [*The Awful Adventures of Herbert de Renich*] (novel) (as Le Sous-Marin "Le Vengeur" [*The Sub-Marine "The Avenger"*] and

La Bataille Invisible [*The Invisible Battle*], *Le Matin*, Sep. 7, 1917-Feb. 12, 1918; rev. 2 vols. as Le Capitaine Hyx [*Captain Hyx*] and La Bataille Invisible, Lafitte, 1920)

30. La Gare Régulatrice (stage play) (*La Scala*, Jan. 16, 1918)

31. Nouvelles Aventures de Chéri-Bibi [*New Adventures of Chéri-Bibi*] (novel; Chéri-Bibi #2) (*Le Matin*, Apr. 18-Aug. 7, 1919; rev. 2 vols. as Pallas et Chéri-Bibi and Fatalitas!, Laffite, 1921)

32. Le Coeur Cambriolé [*The Stolen Heart*] (short story) (*Je Sais Tout*, Jan. 15, 1920)

33. Tue-La-Mort [*Deathslayer*] (novel) (*Le Matin*, Oct. 7-Dec. 30, 1020; rev. 2 vols. as L'Auberge du Petit Chaperon Rouge [*The Inn of The Little Red Riding Hood*] and La Forge des Quatre-Chemins [*The Forge of Quatre-Chemins*], Laffite, 1923)

34. Le Sept de Trèfle [*The Seven of Clubs*] (novel) (*Le Matin*, Sept. 9-Dec. 1, 1921; rev. 2 vols. as L'Enfer Parisien [*The Parisian Hell*] and Toujours Plus Au Fond [*Always Deeper Below*], Lafitte, 1924)

35. Le Crime de Rouletabille [*The Crime of Rouletabille*] (novel; Rouletabille #6) (*Je Sais Tout*, Oct-Nov, 1921; rev. Lafitte, 1923)

36. Rouletabille chez les Bohémiens [*Rouletabille and the Gypsies*] (novel; Rouletabille #7) (*Le Matin*, Oct. 4-Dec. 14, 1922; rev. Lafitte, 1923)

37. La Poupée Sanglante [*The Bloody Puppet*] (novel; Gabriel #1) (*Le Matin* as La Sublime Aventure de Benedict Masson [*Benedict Masson's Sublime Adventure*], July-Aug., 1923; rev. Tallandier, 1924)

38. La Machine à Assassiner [*The Killing Machine*] (novel; Gabriel #2) (*Le Matin* as Gabriel, Aug.-Sep. 1923; rev. Tallandier, 1924)

39. Les Ténébreuses [*The Dark Ones*] (novel) (*Le Matin*, Apr. 12-July 20, 1924; rev. 2 vols. as La Fin d'un Monde [*The End of a World*] and Du Sang sur la Néva [*Blood on the Neva*], Tallandier, 1925)

40. La Farouche Aventure [*The Fierce Adventure*] (novel) (*Le Journal*, July 25-Sep. 13, 1924; Gallimard, 1925)

41. Hardigras (novel) (*Le Journal*, Feb. 19-May 18, 1925; rev. as Le Fils des Trois Pères [*The Son of Three Fathers*], Baudiniere, 1926)

42. Le Noël du Petit Vincent [*The Xmas of Little Vincent*] (short story) (*Cyrano*, Aug. 1924)

43. Not' Olympe (short story) (*Cyrano*, Oct.-Nov. 1924)

44. La Femme au Collier de Velours [*The Woman with a Velvet Necklace*] (short story) (*Cyrano*, 1925)

45. L'Auberge Epouvantable [*The Frightful Inn*] (short story) (*Cyrano*, June 1925)

46. Le Coup d'Etat de Chéri-Bibi [*Chéri-Bibi's Coup d'Etat*] (novel; Chéri-Bibi #3) (as Le Marchand de Cacahouètes [*The Peanut Salesman*], *Le Matin*, Jul. 16-Oct. 4, 1925; rev. Baudinière, 1926)

47. La Mansarde en Or [*The Golden Attic*] (novel) (*Le Journal*, Dec. 11 1925-Jan. 21, 1926)

48. Les Mohicans de Babel [*The Mohicans of Babel*] (novel) (*Le Journal*, July 17-Sept. 19, 1926; rev. Baudinière, 1928)

49. Mister Flow (novel) (*Le Journal*, Jan,. 12-Feb. 25, 1927, Baudinière, 1927)

50. Les Chasseurs de Danse [*The Dance Hunters*] (novel) (*Journal des Voyages*, Jan. 20-Sept 1, 1927; completed by Charles de Richter)

Posthumous publications:

51. L'Agonie de la Russie Blanche [*The Agony of White Russia*] (collection of articles) (Jeanne Gaston-Leroux, 1928)

52. Du Capitaine Dreyfus au Pôle Sud [*From Captain Dreyfus to the South Pole*] (collection of articles) (UGE, 1985)

53. Pouloulou (draft of a novel written c. 1914) (Michel Lafon, 1990)

Authorized sequels:
1. Les Fils de Balaoo [*The Sons of Balaoo*] (by Stanislas-André Steeman) (*Paris-Soir*, 1934; rev. Libr. Champs-Elysées, 1937)
2. Rouletabille contre la Dame de Pique [*Rouletabille vs. The Queen of Spades*] (by Noré Brunel) (*Le Soir*, 1947)
3. Rouletabille Joue et Gagne [*Rouletabille Plays and Wins*] (by Noré Brunel) (*Le Soir*, 1947)

BLACK COAT PRESS

Jean-Marc Lofficier. *The Katrina Protocol*
Jean-Marc & Randy Lofficier. *Edgar Allan Poe on Mars*
Jean-Marc & Randy Lofficier. *Robonocchio*
J.-M. & R. Lofficier (eds.). *Tales of the Shadowmen 1: The Modern Babylon*
J.-M. & R. Lofficier (eds.). *Tales of the Shadowmen 2: Gentlemen of the Night*
J.-M. & R. Lofficier (eds.). *Tales of the Shadowmen 3: Danse Macabre*
J.-M. & R. Lofficier (eds.). *Tales of the Shadowmen 4: Lords of Terror*
Xavier Mauméjean. *The League of Heroes*
Frank J. Morlock. *Sherlock Holmes: The Grand Horizontals*
Marie Nizet. *Captain Vampire*
C. Nodier, Beraud & Toussaint Merle. *Frankenstein*
Charles Nodier. *Lord Ruthven the Vampire*
Henri de Parville. *An Inhabitant of the Planet Mars*
John William Polidori. *Lord Ruthven the Vampire*
P.-A. Ponson du Terrail. *The Vampire and the Devil's Son*
Eugène Scribe. *Lord Ruthven the Vampire*
Brian Stableford. *The New Faust at the Tragicomique*
Brian Stableford. *The Stones of Camelot*
Brian Stableford. *The Wayward Muse*
Brian Stableford (ed.). *News from the Moon*
Villiers de l'Isle-Adam. *The Scaffold*
Villiers de l'Isle-Adam. *The Vampire Soul*
Philippe Ward. *Artahe: The Legacy of Jules de Grandin*
David White: *Fantômas in America*

NON FICTION
Jean-Marc & Randy Lofficier. *Shadowmen: Heroes and Villains of French Pulp Fiction*
Jean-Marc & Randy Lofficier. *Shadowmen 2: Heroes and Villains of French Comics*
Randy Lofficier. *Over Here: An American Expatriate in the South of France*